# Sharing SECRETS

## NATALIE HOTHORNE

Natalie Hothorne Publishing

# Table Of Contents

# Coffee and Old Lovers

**December 20th**

Savanna

The little shop was located three blocks from our hotel. As soon as I opened the door, the intoxicating aroma of freshly ground beans greeted me. Already anticipating that first jolt of bitter sweetness, the tension left my body. Marino's cafe Cubana was almost enough to make me forget how much I was dreading this trip and considered forgiving Josh.

My good mood was short-lived when I spotted the perfect glutes ahead of me in line. It may have been two years, but I still remembered every contour of his perfect ass. I turned to leave, but Brock saw me before I could get to the door.

"Savanna? Is that you?"

Fuck. I turned and gave a halfhearted smile. "Hello Brock. I would love to chat, but I just realized I forgot my wallet at the hotel."

"I see your nose still wiggles when you try to lie." He flashed me a glimpse of his perfect pearl white teeth. "I have missed you, and I know how much you love the coffee here."

Not wanting to make a scene, I got back in line. It had been two years since I saw Brock last, and he was even more beautiful than I remembered. After paying for our coffee, he guided me to a booth in the corner. Sliding across the vinyl bench, I was aware of the dampness between my thighs. Brock has always had that effect on me.

His skin is baked golden brown, like the California desert. Biceps bulge beneath his shirt. Even though the man has never been inside a gym, his physique is flawless. It is the product of demanding work. Tourists have an insatiable appetite for Pink Royals and the nets are heavy. Already knowing the answer, I asked, "Are you still working the Gulf?"

"I just anchored at Stock Island yesterday. She will sit there until the season starts again." I could tell he was already itching to get back on the water. "If I am lucky, I will die on that boat, just like my dad."

I knew he meant it. Brock loves what he does for a living and cannot imagine doing anything else. Which is the reason he is my ex-boyfriend. There is no way I could live this close to my parents, and he would never be happy anywhere else.

"So, how long are you in town?"

"Just for the holiday. If you can call it that."

He was aware of how I felt about the subject. It never snows in Key West. How can you have Christmas without snow? There was five inches on the ground when we flew out of Indianapolis yesterday. But here, there is nothing but sand and sun. It is so hot, even the Santas wear shorts and Hawaiian shirts.

"You don't need to wear stocking caps and gloves for it to feel like Christmas." He stroked the back of my hand, and a jolt ran up my spine. "Would you like to go to the tree lighting tonight?"

"We have plans," I said, moving my hand away. "I did not come alone."

Someone who did not know Brock as well as I do might not have caught the brief flicker of sadness in his eyes. As quickly as it appeared, it was gone, and his affable smile was back. "Are you staying with your parents?"

"God, no." I shudder at the thought. "We have a room at the Beach House."

"Well, I hope he treats you the way you deserve."

"He's a good guy. His name is Josh, and we have been together for about a year. How about you? Anybody special in your life?"

"I see a couple of people now and then, but nothing serious." He tugs at his left ear. And I already know what he is going to say. "Maybe we can get together while you are here. You, me, and your new beau."

An old familiar warmth spreads between my thighs. I try not to think of all the naughty things we did in his house on Caroline. Things I am not sure Josh would approve of. "I don't think that's such a good idea. In fact, I need to get back to the hotel. We have a noon reservation to go jet skiing."

"Jet skiing? I remember a time you would not go near the water."

"What can I say? I'm a different woman from the girl you knew before."

Before leaving the cafe, I looked back and sighed. Regardless of what I had said to Brock, some things had not changed.

Three years ago, at a low point in my life, he was just what I needed. The school district I worked for had to lay off teachers. Since I was one of the last hired, I was among the first they let go. The semester was just about to start, and it was too late to apply elsewhere. When I could not pay my share of the rent, the guy I was living with strongly suggested I find a new place to live. I still don't know what I ever saw in him.

In desperation, I called my mom and dad, hoping they would help me out. Dad said they had an extra room in the main house of the resort. I could stay there rent free until I got back on my feet. He even agreed to pay for my plane ticket. The only catch was my mother's insistence that I help around the resort. I accepted his offer with the understanding I would not have to have any contact with the guests. My responsibilities were limited to the laundry, setting up the breakfast buffet and arranging the Friday evening happy hour.

Still hurting from how lousy my last boyfriend treated me and how much I missed teaching, I spent the time I was not working in my room, reading and feeling sorry for myself. Then I met Brock.

# Brock

I had been friends with Flynn and Rita long before I met their daughter, Savanna. Shrimping is not a year-round profession. From March to December, we work the Gulf for the pinks and the Atlantic for browns. At the end of December, the fishing drops off, and I have two and a half months of free time.

It was the beginning of January, and I was enjoying a beer at Tony's, trying to decide how to spend my time off. The door opened and a lanky gentleman walked in and took a seat next to me. I had never seen him before and just assumed he was another tourist.

He told me his name was Flynn and he and his wife had moved down here six months earlier. We chatted, and he bought me another beer. He had just bought the old Swanson place and planned to turn it into a guest house. I was familiar with the building he was talking about. It had good bones but would require a fair amount of work to make it fit for guests.

"I can do most of the work," he said. "I have been asking around town as to where I might find someone to help me with the heavy stuff. In almost every instance, your name came up."

He seemed like a good guy, and I was flattered he had sought me out. "I would be happy to help you, but just until shrimp season starts up again."

Together we worked every day on the house and finished the renovations by mid-March. On Friday at quitting time, Flynn's wife, Rita, would meet us at the site with a cooler full of beer. Sitting around the empty pool, I heard stories of their daughter and how proud they were of her.

"She sounds like a special woman. I would love to meet her next time she is in town."

"Oh, she never comes to visit," said Rita. Flynn chimed in that she was too busy with school, but I found it odd that she did not at least come for the holidays. Most locals cannot keep their northern relatives away.

It would be two more years before I met Savanna and fell in love for the first time in my life.


It was a Friday; the night Flynn and Rita treated their guests to a happy hour. I usually provided them with a crate of that day's catch. Normally, one of my crew made the delivery on their way home. But everyone had plans that night, so I decided to drop it off myself.

When I walked through the back door, her back was to me, and I must have surprised her. She turned around and gave out a little squeak, almost falling on her cute butt.

In the yellow tank top and tight jean shorts, she was a perfect likeness of Rita. The same auburn hair, which looked even redder against the milky white flesh of her shoulders. The same small, compact frame as her mom, but twenty years younger, her heavy breasts still rode high and tight.

"You must be Savanna." Stepping into the kitchen, I said, "I have heard so much about you. Good to see you have finally come for a visit."

Regaining her composure, she gave me a steely look. "Who are you, and what are you doing in my kitchen?"

Showing her the crate in my arms, I said, "I am Brock and I'm delivering your shrimp."

"I didn't order any shrimp," she continued to eye me with distrust.

Flynn came into the kitchen, sparing me any further interrogation. "Leave him alone. It is rare for a boat captain to deliver our seafood personally." He gave me a wink. "I am going to turn on the pool lights. Tell Hank we said hello."

"Who's Hank?"

"My partner."

Savanna smiled for the first time and apologized for her rudeness. She said she mistook me for a guest. I got the idea she had a low opinion of her parents' business.

The more we talked, and she explained the circumstances that had brought her to Key West, I realized how unhappy she was at Mango Cove and desperately needed an evening of fun. "Have you ever been to the drag show?"

"No," then she gave me a shy smile. "But it sounds interesting."

"I know a couple of girls in the cast. They can get us a table down front for tonight's performance. If you are free."

"Let me check my calendar," she said, leafing through a stack of takeout menus. "I imagine Mama Q's can live without me for one night."

"Great. I will meet you here at 8:00. We can have dinner before the show."

Even today, knowing how things turned out, I would do it all over again. But this time I would open up to her, be more expressive. Two years is a long time to live with a broken heart. I have learned how to show my feelings, but it is too late. She is back but has a boyfriend with her.

I can't help but wonder what Josh is like. He must be someone special for Savanna to have let him into her life.

## Savanna-Three Years Earlier

Just my luck. The first interesting man I meet since landing on this damn island, and he is gay. It is probably for the best. I am not ready for another relationship, but it will be nice to hang out with a man I can be myself with. No sexual tension to get in the way. Once I finish setting up for happy hour, I go to my room and shower.

I am excited to be going out. Even though he has nothing beyond a platonic interest in me, my body is tingling. The man was sexy as fuck, and for the first time since leaving Indianapolis, I was horny.

Stepping into the shower, I try to imagine what he looks like beneath his long sleeve t-shirt and baggy, board shorts. Soaping my breasts, my thoughts soon run wild. I imagine him kissing Hank. They are both nude. My hand dips between my thighs while thinking of the two men fondling each other. I give out a soft moan. In my fantasy, Brock is on his knees, Hank in his mouth. The image is so hot, it only takes a couple of flicks of my finger against the hard bud to put me over the edge.

My heart was still beating rapidly when I toweled off. It was not the first time I had fantasized about two men. In fact, it is one of my favorite scenarios to use when pleasuring myself.

I looked in the small dresser. The only clothes I brought from home are shorts and tank tops. Tonight, called for something dressier. Checking my mother's closet, I consider the blue and pink floral sun dress. It is backless and I won't be able to wear a bra. After a moment's hesitation, I decided to go for it. No one will be looking at me, anyway.

I was waiting out front when Brock arrived. He looked gorgeous. The deep tanned skin of his muscular thighs contrasted with the bright white of his shorts and the faded pink polo stretched across his broad chest. His chestnut brown hair was slightly tousled. The casual look was a popular one in Key West, but he made it work on a completely new level. Flashing me his perfect teeth, "You look amazing."

"You clean up pretty good yourself." I grinned at him. "Where are we headed—Captain?"

"When we are on shore, you can call me Brock," he said with a twinkle in his soft brown eyes. Then he asked what I felt like eating. I told him anything but seafood or pizza. My parents seem to have fish at every meal, and I was burned out on delivery from Mama Q's.

"I know the perfect place," he said, taking my hand and leading the way.

It was the first chance I had to see the town at night. The streets were crowded with tourists. We were bathed in the electric glow of the colorful signs that hung above the many bars lining Duval.

Music came from the open doors of every bar we passed. I did not know what I had been missing by hiding out in my room at Mango Cove. Grateful to be out of my parents' house, I gave Brock's hand a soft squeeze.

"Here we are."

According to the plaque on the wall, the building was the former home of a sea captain and his family in the 1800s. It now housed a steakhouse. Brock asked if I wanted to eat inside, but I was looking at the tables set up in the alley between the restaurant and the neighboring building. Bare bulbs hung beneath cloth sails. There was a man playing acoustic guitar on a small stage. Best of all, there was a cool breeze blowing. When the hostess greeted us, Brock asked for a table on the patio.

Over appetizers, we got to know one other better. Brock had lived in Key West his entire life. The son and grandson of fishermen, his family had been making a living from the waters surrounding the island for generations.

I wondered aloud why he had stayed in Key West for so long. He was intelligent, witty, and charming as hell.

"The people. The feeling of community and acceptance. I am sure there are friendly folks everywhere, but I cannot imagine there is a more colorful cast of characters anywhere. I can be who I am, and no one thinks twice about it."

"I guess I can understand what you mean. There is no way my parents could have opened a place like Mango Cove back in Indianapolis. Thank God."

"You really don't approve of your parents' lifestyle, do you?"

"Do you mean, do I wish they didn't sleep with other people? Of course I do. Any kid would prefer that their parents be monogamous. But it is their lives and how they get their jollies is none of my business."

"Then why do you seem to resent them so much?"

He was a good listener and did not interrupt as I told him about the circumstances that had brought me here and my strained relationship with my parents.

"When I was young, they were two of the most loving people I have ever met. They preached the importance of family, honesty, and trust."

He nodded. "That sounds like Rita and Flynn. So, what is the problem?"

"Every October, they would take a vacation. Just the two of them. I was never invited. When I got older, I asked to go along. My mother has always been big on honesty and felt compelled to tell me the truth. They came down here for an annual swinger event."

He said he knew the festival I was talking about and asked how my mother's revelation made me feel.

"I was confused by it at first. I mean, who wouldn't be if they found out their parents were hooking up with other people? Eventually I got over the yuck factor and just ignored it. What they did on vacation was none of my business."

But after I graduated high school, they sold the house and announced they were moving to Key West. I was hurt and angry. It felt like they were choosing their friends over me. "Who does that? Abandons their child and moves halfway across the country?"

"It does not sound to me like they abandoned you. When you had a setback, they opened their home and gave you a place to live until you get back on your feet."

"Well, when you put it that way, it makes me sound pretty selfish." But he was not done.

"It sounds like you have had a rather good life. Both your parents adore you." He hesitated, tugging his ear before continuing. "My mom took off when I was thirteen. She was not from the keys and said she always felt like an outsider. Dad and I never heard from her after she left.

Taking his hand in mine, "I am so sorry that happened to you. It makes my life sound rather good by comparison."

He waved me off. "It was a long time ago. My point is your parents love you, and that did not change just because they have a new address."

"I can see why my dad likes you so much. You have made me look at my parents in a whole new light." The waitress brought our plates.

As we ate, the conversation returned to happier topics and soon we were both laughing. I thought, not for the first time, what a shame it was he is gay. I could really fall for a man like him. Hank was a lucky guy.

Halfway through my rib-eye, I glanced across the street. I took a closer look before asking, "Are those men dancing on the bar over there?"

Without looking up from his seafood risotto, Brock said, "Probably. It is about the time the go-go boys start. How is your steak?"

I took another bite and assured him it was fabulous. He saw me looking through the open window at the dancers.

"It's a gay bar. They dance for tips."

"Do you and Hank go there?"

"I do, but it really isn't Hank's thing. I go by myself." That made me angry. I had been burned by too many cheaters in my young life to be friends with one. "So, you just go there to hook up with random strangers while he sits at home? Is that it?"

"Leave who at home?" He tugged at his left ear, surprised by the change in my tone.

"Your partner. Hank."

His laughter drew looks from the other diners. "Hank is my business partner. He owns a share of my boat, the *Gulf Queen*."

My face flushed. "So, Hank isn't your lover?" He shook his head. 'You must think I am a fool, flying off the handle like that."

"Not at all." he snickered, "I can see how you misunderstood."

"I'm sorry I accused you of being a cheater. I've had boyfriends who cheated, so infidelity is a hot button for me."

"I see that," he said with a laugh. "The funny thing is, Hank is straight as they come. Wait until I tell him you thought we were lovers."

I groaned.

"And for the record, I am not gay either. I am bisexual."

"Oh. I see." The implications played in my head.

After that first evening, my time in Key West no longer felt like a prison sentence. Daily chores no longer seemed like work and even though my mother could still push my buttons, I did not let it ruin my feelings of happiness.

Brock seemed to sense what I needed and when I needed it. If I had a rough day, we would watch the sunset and he would point out how small my problems were in the grand scheme of things. He made me laugh, like the night he took me to a karaoke bar. He must have sung every song from the musical Hamilton, each more out of tune than the one before. I appreciated his enthusiasm. The man had a joy for life that was contagious.

My feelings quickly extended beyond friendship. When I was with him, my heart would flutter. I felt empty inside If I did not see him for a couple of days. I could not imagine my life without Brock in it.

The first time he invited me to his home, I turned him down, knowing what would happen if we were alone. My desires had grown beyond my brain's ability to stifle my physical needs, and I wanted nothing to ruin our perfect friendship. With no intention of staying in Key West, it would be stupid for me to get involved in a serious relationship.

Later that evening, lying in my lonely bed, I was filled with regret at having turned down his invitation. I wanted to feel his body against mine. Skin on skin. To hell with the consequences. I had not been so aroused by a man in a very long time. I touched myself, hoping to relieve some of the pent-up desire, but it was pointless. Release eluded me. I wanted to be with Brock, and my hand proved to be a poor substitute.

The next morning, I heard pounding outside my window. Dad was on top of the pool house, repairing a spot where some shingles had come loose. Brock was helping him. I watched him carry the shingles up the ladder. His biceps were bulging under the heavy load. When finished, he removed his shirt and wiped beads of perspiration from his muscular chest. My heart was racing. I briefly considered going back to bed and pleasuring myself. But knew it would not satisfy my burning desire. I wanted more, needed much more.

I dressed in a hurry, pulling on my shortest shorts and tightest tank top. Rather than taking time to do my hair, I pulled it back into a ponytail and grabbed a couple of bottles of icy water from the kitchen.

"Bless you sweet child." Dad said, coming down from the roof. "It's thirsty work out here." He pressed the bottle to the back of his neck and moved into the shade.

When he was out of hearing distance, I leaned into Brock and asked, "Is that invitation to dinner still good?"

He looked down, taking in every curve of my body. Then asked, "Does tonight work for you?"

Brock lived on a quiet side street; in the home he had grown up in. Unlike the other houses on the street, his was freshly painted. The front yard was small but well kept. Palm fronds whispered in the light breeze, and I panicked.

It was a mistake to come here. If I went through with this, it would change everything between Brock and me. I did not want to jeopardize my only friendship. The door opened just as I turned to leave. Brock casually leaned against the doorway. "Dinner's almost ready. Are you coming in?"

I hesitated, not sure if it was the aroma of food or Brock's taut body making my mouth water. "Is that bacon I smell?"

"I wrapped the shrimp in it." That settled it. Bacon makes everything better.

The inside of his house was just as neat as the outside. Grabbing a few things from a small kitchen, he guided me to the backyard. We nibbled on the shrimp while he grilled steaks. Over dinner, I asked him about the books in his living room. One entire wall was taken up by bookshelves. Brock explained that he never went to college, but it did not mean he could not educate himself. The teacher in me found that admirable, and a little sexy.

The nervousness I felt earlier faded as we talked. We both knew the reason I was there, but he did not rush me. In fact, I was wondering if I had done something to change his mind. Then, as I was helping him clean up, he wrapped his arms around my waist and nuzzled my neck.

When I turned to face him, he slipped a finger beneath my chin, tilting my face towards his. Eyes the color of the waters surrounding this tiny piece of paradise stared back at me. Eyes that seemed to know everything I was thinking. A shiver ran through my body when he touched the back of my neck. His lips were soft, and I could taste the remnants of salt on his tongue.

Never had my senses been so alive. I heard and felt everything around me. The swish of palm fronds rubbing together, just beyond the open window. A slight breeze, cool against my hot skin. The scent of lilacs and jasmine. Brock's soft touch, raising goose bumps on my flesh.

Lips now mashing together, we stood in that tiny kitchen, hands exploring one another. He smelled of limes and sea spray. Lost in his embrace, I could have been content to go on like that forever.

But then I felt his hardness press against me, and my body demanded the pleasures it had for so long been denied. I jumped into his arms and let him carry me to the bedroom. Our explorations became more feverish. Brock's soft lips did not leave mine as we undressed. Once we were both nude, he stepped back.

Stripped bare and vulnerable, standing before this perfect specimen of manhood should have made me uncomfortable. But what I saw in his eyes was not naked lust. It was adoration. Any insecurities I felt about my body faded when he said, "You are beautiful. I want you more than I have ever wanted anyone."

Kissing his soft mouth, I whispered, "Don't tell me. Show me."

My breasts are rather large and a source of embarrassment. But Brock seemed enthralled by them. His finger traced the rim of my wide areolas, causing them to quickly pebble. With a soft moan, I put a hand behind his neck, guiding his mouth to my erect nipple. Taking it between his lips, he gently massaged my other breast. I gave out another moan, this one slightly louder.

My heartbeat faster when Brock kissed and sucked his way down my torso. I ran my fingers through his thick head of hair, while he layered soft kisses across my belly. Eager to feel his mouth on me, I urged him lower. My breath caught when he paused and ran a finger across the small patch of fur just above my labia. "I want to taste you. Would that be all right?"

"Yes. Oh yes — please." I gasped and spread my legs wide.

Brock traced along the line of my seam. A long 'fuck, yes,' escaped my lips. My moans grew louder with each pass of his tongue. The more he moved up and down my rapidly parting lips, the greater my need to feel a piece of him inside me. "Put your finger in me," I was almost begging.

I cried out in surprise when he quickly found my G-spot. By the time his mouth was on my pulsing nub, I was grasping at the sheets. Writhing in ecstasy, the first wave washed across my body. I cried out. "You are amazing."

Brock seemed determined to give me as many orgasms as I could handle. Every time I came down from a high, he would change directions and coax another burst of pleasure from my still quivering body. Finally, I could take no more and pulled him up to me.

I was still trying to catch my breath. "Brock, that was incredible."

"Why did you stop me? I was enjoying myself. You taste so good, and I love the little squeaking noise you make right before you come."

I playfully slapped his shoulder and giggled. "I do not squeak, besides even if I do, it's not polite to point it out."

"I guess I will have to listen closer this time." He pinned my wrists above my head and kissed me deeply. He was growing harder against my twitching loins. Neither of us could wait any longer. He released my hands. Reaching between our fervid bodies, I grasped his shaft and guided him to my hunger. "I want you so badly, but it has been a long time. Please be gentle."

"I will be." His eyes never leaving mine, he slowly inched forward. My body tingled with bliss. As he moved deeper, I gasped, and he paused causing me to cry out, "Don't stop now."

Wanting his entire length, I gripped his firm buttocks and drew him deeper. When he reached my depth, he held himself in place. Hands on my shoulders, he leaned down. My eyelids fluttered beneath his soft kisses. Then, with a fiery passion, he kissed me on the mouth. My hips twisted and turned, my needy pussy pulsing around his thickness, demanding attention.

We moved together, and I felt an electric jolt shoot through my body, like nothing I had ever experienced before. I knew from the look in his eyes, I was not the only one to feel it. It was as if our bodies were a perfect fit for one another. Every contour, designed to bring maximum pleasure. Every movement, increasing desire, pulling us closer and closer.

My senses were alive, and I felt an intense awareness spread over me. I felt every beat of his heart. Heard every breath he took. Felt every ridge of his fingers moving over my flesh. The taste of his salty flesh strong on my lips.

An electrified pulse began humming in my core. Growing in intensity, it spread across my body, drowning out every other sensation.

Chests heaving, we made love as if our lives depended on it. Eyes never leaving one another's. Brock's cock swelled with each thrust. Wanting to feel every bit of him, I clenched the tight muscles of my pussy and bore down.

Despite how incredible it felt, I could not wait any longer for release and whispered, "Come with me, Brock." He spasmed and the orgasm which had been building since the night I met him released. Holding him tight, I cried real tears.

Brock looked at me with concern in his soft eyes. "Are you all right?"

Sweat was pouring from our bodies, I was panting, and tears continued to flow down my cheeks. I assured him I was fine. "I've just never come that hard before." He kissed me, softly this time.

Eventually, he rolled off and pulled me close. I laid my head on his chest, until I felt myself getting sleepy. I got up and dressed. "You are welcome to spend the night."

I told him I appreciated the offer but did not want a hundred questions from mother in the morning. When he offered to walk me home, I reminded him it was just a couple of blocks, and I would be fine.

I needed to get away from him and clear my head. Even though he had given me the best orgasm of my life, it was not the real reason for my tears. I was falling in love with him.

There was no future for us. Brock loved the life he had built in Key West. I knew he would never leave and I could not imagine myself ever getting used to the constant heat and humidity. It was ridiculous to think things between us could ever work.

Against my better judgment, we continued to see each other. He never seemed to grow tired of my company but said nothing to make me believe his feelings were as strong as mine. It did not matter, he made me happy, and I was willing to take whatever affection he gave. For the first time in my life, I was living in the moment, not worrying about the future.

My heart was not the only thing I opened to Brock. I believed he was open-minded and shared my fantasies with him. He was receptive. These were things I had fantasized about, but never dreamed I would get to try. I thought he was as turned on by the idea as I was. But looking back, I realize what we did made him see me in a different light. Not a good one.

When I first came to stay with my parents, I tried to find a teaching position in the, and quickly discovered there were no openings, even for substitutes. Teaching is my passion, and I hated living with my parents, so I began sending resumes to schools back home. I heard nothing back for months. When I told Brock I had received a job offer in Indianapolis, all he said was, "It sounds like a wonderful opportunity."

It broke my heart. I had hoped he would say he loved me and ask me to stay. But, he did not see me that way, and it was my fault. I should never have shared my fantasies with him. I assumed he was into it, but it ruined our relationship. In his mind I was no longer the woman he thought I was.

I called the principal to accept the position and booked a return flight home. My time with Brock was a learning experience. If ever I opened my heart to another man, my fantasies, and kinky desires would remain locked away forever.

In the week leading up to my flight, I hid out in my room at Mango Cove. As far as I know, Brock never tried to contact me.

When it was time to leave for the airport on Saturday, I was in a sour mood. The weekends are the busiest time for Mango Cove, with new guests checking in and old ones checking out. My mother was checking people in behind the registration desk. I did not stop to say goodbye. Dad had just finished putting my last piece of luggage in the trunk of the Buick.

"Not that I mind taking my favorite daughter to the airport, but I thought maybe Brock would take you."

"I am your only daughter. And he offered, but I turned him down." I got in and buckled my seatbelt. Even with the traffic, it was only a 10-minute ride to the airport. I am sure my father realized I didn't feel like talking. But that did not stop him.

"I have known Brock for a long time, and he is quick to lend a sympathetic ear to your problems, but he's not one to talk about his own feelings. It doesn't mean he doesn't have them, and I can tell by the way he looks at you he has them."

"Not anymore," I said. If my dad wondered what had happened, he did not ask. He was rather good about respecting my privacy but even if he had asked there was no way I would tell him what really happened. After all, it was his nonsensical philosophy on ethical non-monogamy that had encouraged me to first broach the subject with Brock.

Eventually, I got over the pain and fell in love with Josh, but I never forgot the promise I had made myself. Seeing Brock in the coffee shop today brought back a little of the hurt. But what made me most uncomfortable was the burning desire I felt in my loins.

# New Beginnings

Savanna

After leaving Key West, I arrived in Indianapolis a week before the semester was about to begin. My new apartment was old and outdated. I had leased it sight unseen when the principal called and offered me my old job back. It was all I could afford to pay in rent Although my parents covered my expenses in Key West, I still had a ton of credit card debt to pay off.

Aside from the water heater occasionally going out, it was not a bad apartment. Surely better than living with my parents.

I was glad to be back in the classroom. My Advanced English students were engaged and kept me too busy to think about Brock. I could have dated if I wanted, there was no shortage of men asking me out, but I turned them down. I was not ready for another relationship.

Time flew by quickly and the semester was drawing to an end. By that point I had gotten to know the other tenants. I was coming home from work when Mrs. Hanshaw called to me. She was a lonely old lady who loved to gossip. Normally I would stop and let her prattle on, but I was tired. It had been a long day. I just wanted to take a shower and make dinner. I pretended to not hear her and started up the steps."

"The new building manager was asking about you today."

That stopped in my tracks. I had seen the man a couple of times. He was sexy in a dad bod kind of way. I caught him checking me out once and pretended not to notice. There was something about the way he looked at me. It made me tingly inside. I had to remind myself I was not ready to date.

Mrs. Hanshaw must have seen the look on my face because she said, "Oh don't worry, I didn't tell him anything about you."

"I appreciate that." But I was sure the man had heard everything the old woman knew about me, which really wasn't that much. Still, I made a mental note to avoid him. I saw no need to put temptation in front of me. And he was tempting.

"You know he's single? He grew up in Indianapolis and is a college graduate." She winked at me. "Good job and very handsome."

Her shoulders slumped when I said, "Thank you, but I'm not looking to date anyone right now."


Josh


I was a couple of weeks into the new job when a tenant on the fourth floor called me to complain about a leaky faucet. I was on my way to their unit when I caught my first glimpse of Savanna. She was the most beautiful woman I had ever seen. Eyes the color of emeralds, long reddish hair, and a figure her tight sweater could not hide. I did not know her name or which apartment she lived in, but I knew two things. I was in lust, and she was out of my league.

After graduating college, I wasted my twenties; partying and bouncing from job to job, trying to find something that would make me happy. When the gig economy came along, it seemed perfect. I became an independent contractor in the food industry.

Which is a fancy way of saying, I was a driver for a takeout delivery service. It may not have been glamorous, but I was my own boss, only taking assignments when I wanted to. If I didn't feel like going to work, nobody hassled me.

The problem was, if I did not work, they didn't pay me. I was about a month away from ending up on my mother's couch, when I decided I needed a real job. My degree was in property management, but you would be surprised how few opportunities there are for 30-year-old men, with no stable work history.

The old man who owned the apartment building, did not care about such things. For what he was paying, he could not be too picky. I only took the job because it included free rent, and I was about to be evicted from my previous apartment.

A busybody tenant, who stayed up on such things, happily informed me the woman of my desire had moved into C-12 six months earlier. She was a teacher and was trying to get back on her feet. Because it is an old building, the rent is cheap. The low price comes at a cost, however. There are forty units, and it seems like I spend all my time making repairs.

After a frustrating day spent handling tenant complaints, all I wanted to do was microwave my dinner and have a beer. Instead, there was a steady knocking at my door. Whoever it was, showed no signs of giving up.

I ripped the door open and growled, "What is so important, you need to interrupt my dinner for?" I regretted losing my temper. It was the girl from C-12, wearing an incredibly short robe. Her auburn hair matted with shampoo.

"Let me guess, no hot water." She nodded. "I'll get my toolbox."

It did not take me long to figure out the pilot light had gone out, but instead of re-lighting it, I pretended to study the control panel. It was rare that I got invited to an attractive woman's apartment. And this one was sexier than most.

She was leaning over my shoulder and the scent of her coconut body wash, was making me horny. "Are you sure it's not the pilot light?"

"These old units can be tricky," I said looking back at her. She had not tied the robe tight enough and gifted me with a view of her incredible breasts. I quickly returned my eyes to the water heater but knew I would be thinking about those milky orbs later that night.

She said she would give me space to work, while she rinsed her hair out. When she was gone, I saw no need to continue my charade and lit the pilot light. I stayed in the utility closet a few more minutes, wanting to make sure the water got hot and give my erection time to go down.

I was putting my tools away when she came out of the bathroom, her hair wrapped in a towel and the robe now cinched around her slender waist. "I don't know what you did, but the water is already getting warm."

"Okay, I am going to get back to my dinner then."

"Do you mean the frozen heart attack in a box, you were about to microwave, when I showed up at your door?"

"They are quick and easy." I said defensively.

"And loaded with sodium." She wiggled her nose. "I appreciate you coming up so quickly. The old building manager would have taken days to get it fixed. Why don't you stay for dinner? I'm making pasta marinara."

I could not tell whether she was coming on to me or just a nice person. Either way, a home cooked meal sounded good, and I was hoping to catch another glimpse of what was under that robe.

"Great. Just let me change quick and then I will start dinner."

Her apartment was much neater than mine. She had three shelves filled with books; their spines lined up perfectly straight. I am not a big reader myself, but on the top shelf I saw many of the same classics I had been forced to read in school. Dickens, Hemingway, Steinbeck, books you would expect an English teacher to read.

The middle shelf held textbooks on assorted topics of education. I was surprised by the titles on the bottom shelf. Savanna came into the living room as I was thumbing through one of the paperbacks. I was disappointed to see a baggy sweatshirt and yoga pants had replaced the robe.

"I see you found my guilty pleasure," she laughed. "Promise you will not tell. I don't need the parents knowing their kid's teacher is a closet smut reader."

"I shall take your secret to my death, me lady."

She laughed and touched my arm, but I did not get my hopes up. Her hair was in a ponytail and the workout clothes made it less likely she was coming on to me.

I wish I could tell you I discovered what an amazing person she was and fell in love that night. The truth was, I just hoped to get laid. Commitment scared me. Which is why I preferred to meet people on hook-up apps. At that time, I had only been in one committed relationship, and it had ended poorly.

Savanna was an excellent cook and very funny. She loved teaching, and it showed in the way she talked about her students. Once dinner was over, I was thinking I might have a chance to get her in bed and looked for a reason to stay. "Dinner was terrific. Let me help you clean up."

"Nonsense, I will get it after I brush out my hair. Thanks, again for fixing the water heater so quickly." It was clear she was ready for me to leave.

My cock was aching as I retreated downstairs. As soon as I locked my door, I climbed into bed. Already picturing Savanna nude, I wrapped my hand around my shaft and stroked to the image of her amazing tits.

A week later, Savanna was coming home from work at the same time I had just returned from the grocery store. "Hey stranger." She gave me a smile as she opened the front door for us.

"That is a lot of frozen dinners," she said eying my bags. "Don't you ever cook?"

"Sometimes," I lied. "It's just not worth the hassle for one person."

"I understand, believe me I do. But those things are so bad for you." She paused and her nose gave the cutest little wiggle. "I hate cooking for just me as much as you do. Why don't I make enough for both of us tonight."

"Only if you let me help. I don't want you thinking I can't cook."

"It's a date then." she said, "I will see you in a couple of hours."


My mind was reeling. Had she meant what she said? Was it really a date? And if so, did that mean we were going to have sex? Just to be on the safe side after showering and shaving, I put on my lucky underwear.

When she opened the door, wearing sweats, I wondered why I had spent so much time deciding what shirt to wear. Even in sweatpants her ass looked amazing. I followed her to the kitchen. "What can I do to help with dinner?"

"We're having fajitas." She handed me some vegetables and a large knife. "Would you mind slicing the onions and peppers?"

Confident I had seen enough cooking shows to do a passable job, I took the knife.. "What do you teach?" I asked while trying to get the skin off an onion.

"High school English." She was seasoning the chicken.

"Do you enjoy it?" Wanting to impress her, I continued to slice the pepper, without looking down at the cutting board. The way I had seen chefs on TV do it.

"I love it. Are you sure you are okay over there?" Tears were running down my cheeks.

"These onions are super strong," I said trying to hide the fact I had sliced my finger instead of the jalapeño.

"Oh my god, you're bleeding."

As the cut filled with jalapeño juice, I gritted my teeth. "It is possible I overstated my culinary skills."

She had me run my hand under cold water while she went to get a Band-aid. There was a small, framed photograph on a shelf above the sink. Three people, taken at sunset. The man was tall and skinny, his short hair peppered with gray. His arms around two women who looked so much alike, it was obvious they were mother and daughter. I could not help but notice Savanna's smile in the photo looked forced.

While she was applying the band-aid to my wound, I asked her if the picture had been taken on vacation.

"I would not call living with my parents a vacation." She wiggled her nose. "They live in Key West. I spent a year with them."

The idea of living somewhere it never got cold sounded like paradise. No sidewalks to shovel, no chipping ice off your windshield. "Why did you come back?"

"It is complicated." I waited for her to continue. "You need to elevate that hand. Have a seat at the counter while I finish making dinner."

That is how it is with Savanna. If she does not want to talk about something, she will change the subject. We have been together almost a year now and I still do not know why she left Key West.

28

## Savanna

When I met Josh, I was still in love with Brock and had no intention of starting a new relationship. I told him I was not ready for anything beyond friendship. I could tell he was disappointed, but he seemed to accept it. Unlike the other men who asked me out, he was not pushy and respected my privacy. He was one of the good guys.

Not as attractive as the men I usually dated, he made up for it by being a good listener and hilarious. There was something about his self-deprecating humor I found attractive.

It started innocently enough. We lived in the same building and like most single people, I hated cooking just for myself. Josh was a horrible cook and usually ate microwave dinners. It only seemed logical to invite him to share meals with me. At first it was just a couple times a week. We would chat over dinner, sharing the highlight of our days with one another. I avoided talking about my family or any mention of Brock, but Josh shared a great deal with me.

He had two older sisters; one was a lawyer the other a doctor. Like him, they still lived in Indianapolis. Every Sunday, he and his sisters would gather at their parents' house for a family dinner. As an only child, I envied the close relationship he had with his family.

From what he told me, I gathered he had never been in a serious relationship. His job as property manager of the building we both lived in, was his first real job. Something I found surprising, being that he was already in his early thirties. He was much better than the manager they had when I moved in. I am not sure he enjoyed the work, but he took it serious. It was another thing I liked about him.

After a month, we were eating dinner together five nights a week. I cooked while Josh sat at the counter and watched. From time to time, he would try to help, but I preferred he stay out of the kitchen. His cooking skills were atrocious.

We shared a love of old thriller movies. On nights I did not have papers to grade, I would invite him to stay after dinner and we would watch a movie. We sat on my couch munching popcorn and watching movies like, *Killing The Sacred Deer* and *Mulholland Drive*. Every time something in a movie startled me, I would spill the popcorn and Josh would always laugh. He has a great laugh and I love the way he takes joy in even the smallest things. I thought less and less about Brock and more about Josh.

I was making chicken salads for dinner. Josh was in his usual place at the counter, and I was telling him an amusing story about one of the older teachers I work with. When he laughed, his long blonde hair fell across those mischievous hazel eyes, he gave a flick of his head.

That was when I realized I had misjudged how attractive he is. How could I have missed the sensuous lines of his full lips and strong chin? The sexy stubble on his jaw. The muscles beneath his T-shirt. The scent of sandalwood and pepper, which made me want to taste him. I had overlooked it all.

After that night, whenever Josh tried to help in the kitchen, I sent him back to his place at the counter. Not because he is a mess in the kitchen but because the space is a small one and every time our bodies brushed together, my desire would surge.

Josh gave no sign of being affected, but several times when we bumped together, I could feel the hardness pressing against me. I needed him to make the first move. I went so far as bending over the counter, hoping he would take the hint. But night after night, he would return to his apartment, leaving me frustrated.

By the time he left for the evening I was so wound up, I pulled out my vibrator. I was going through batteries so quick; I ordered a rechargeable one from the Passions' website. But even that did not quell the growing ache in loins.

I knew it was my fault. When we first met, I made it clear I was not looking for a physical relationship. Josh had no reason to believe I had changed my mind, and it was becoming clear I would need to take the initiative.

On Friday after dinner, I put on *The Big Easy*. Neither one of us said anything during the scene where Dennis Quaid goes down on Ellen Barkin, but my pussy was aching with want. The bulge in Josh's trousers was larger than normal. I licked my lips and allowed my gaze to move over his body. Hunger was building within me. Hunger for Josh and I could not remember why I had delayed sleeping with this beautiful man for so long.

In the two months he and I had been hanging out, I gave him little reason to believe I had changed my mind about wanting a physical relationship. To say he was surprised would be an understatement.

His eyes went wide, but he did not say a word when I put my hand on his thigh. There was a slight groan when I moved my hand higher on his leg. When my hand reached his cock, he gave out another groan. To his credit he gave me a chance to stop. Looking me in the eye, he asked, "Are you sure you want to do this?"

My response was to crawl on his lap and kiss him. I knew he had been fantasizing about a moment like this since we first met.

Neither of us had been laid in six months and with our hips pressing together, we were beyond capacity for reasoned thought.

When I kissed him, he returned it with equal enthusiasm. Josh traced the soft bow of my lips with the tip of his tongue before nipping at my lower lip. Our tongues entwined, heat radiated from my body, pressed tight against his.

When I broke our kiss and leaned back, I saw the look of disappointment in his eyes, thinking I had changed my mind. But instead of moving from his lap, I looked him in the eyes, "It's getting hot in here." Grabbing the hem of my hoodie, I pulled it over my head, and discarded it to the floor. "That's better."

Before he had time to more than glimpse the flesh spilling over the top of my red bra, I reached behind my neck and moved my hair out of the way. Hoping Josh got the message, I pulled him to me. When he kissed my shoulder, I rewarded him with a contented sigh. His lips were soft and cool against my fevered flesh. He worked his way up my neck. When he reached my ear, I gave out a giggle and pulled away. "That tickles."

A hand at the back of his head, I guided him to a favorite spot. "Try here instead."

As he kissed along my collar bone; my breathing quickened. When he reached my bra strap, he followed its path downward, and a shiver ran up my back. I did not stop him when he released the four snaps at the back, but pressed my arms tight against my body, securing it in place.

The guest house my parents own is clothing optional. My mother loves to sunbathe nude. Although people say we look alike, I do not have the confidence in my body that she has. I am always uncomfortable when people see me topless for the first time. My breasts are not perfectly round and the left one is larger than the right. My petite frame makes them look even larger than they are.

Taking a deep breath, and closing my eyes, I gave a little shimmy. The bra fell loose, and I heard him gasp. When I opened my eyes, he was staring at my chest, his mouth agape. Embarrassed, I covered myself. He pulled my arms back down. "They are even more spectacular than even I imagined."

Breathing a sigh of relief, I arched my back and shook out my hair. My areolas pebbled at his touch. He took one in each of his warm hands, as if testing their heft and massaged the firm flesh. When I moaned, "Use your mouth," he pulled me to him and buried his face in my generous cleavage.

I let out a contented sigh when his lips found my nipple and sucked it between his lips, shooting pleasure to my core. He bit down, setting me ablaze with indescribable rapture. I needed to touch him.

My hands found his zipper, but his straining cock made it difficult. Lifting his hips Josh helped me free him from his jeans before returning his attention to my heaving chest.

My breath caught when I reached into his shorts, and I felt how hard he was. Josh let out a grunt of encouragement. I moved up and down his sizable length. Wanting to feel him in my mouth, I lowered myself to the floor, but he stopped me. "It has been a long time and I am afraid if you do that, the party will be over before it starts."

I whined, and he said, "Why don't we move to the bedroom?"

Hesitating, I tried to remember if I had made the bed and put my dirty clothes in the hamper that morning. His hands cupped my ass and my concerns about housekeeping faded. I took his hand and led him into my bedroom, leaving the lights off just in case.

Josh wasted no time, removing my yoga pants and boy shorts. As soon as he had me naked, he lifted me onto the bed and picked up where he had left off. But he did not stop with my breasts this time.

He kissed, sucked, and nipped his way down my torso. My stomach fluttered when it realized where he was heading. I thought of stopping him, the way he had stopped me in the living room. Tell him it was unfair. But the idea quickly died.

It was as if his fingers and tongue knew exactly where to go and when they should be there. Thought became impossible. Luckily, my body responded instinctively. I may have momentarily lost consciousness.

After the last orgasm faded, I opened my eyes to see Josh lying next to me. "Where did you learn how to do that?" Before he could respond, I quickly said, "Never mind. I don't want to know."

I had never orgasmed so much or so easily from oral sex. Especially the first time I was with someone. Usually there is a lot of fumbling, trial and error and I am left frustrated, but not tonight. It was as if somebody had given Josh a copy of the owner's manual for my body and he had spent weeks studying.

"If you liked that, you are going to love what comes next," he said with a smile.

"Don't get cocky, lover boy." I spread my thighs and pulled him atop me.


Already slick, eager to feel him inside me, I reached between us and guided him to my opening. I let out a gasp as he pushed inward and felt myself open up for him. Oh, how I had missed that feeling.

He stopped and drew back until he was almost out, I whined in exasperation. Then he slid back in again, a little deeper this time. His hips rocking from side to side, Josh slowly drew back before thrusting a little deeper. The feeling already had me on edge. His pelvic bone brushed against my hard nub and I let out a howl of pleasure.

Wanting to feel the sensation again, I grabbed his ass and thrust my hips. My already stimulated body responded quickly. I do not always orgasm as easily as I did that night, but once I have the first one, others seem to flow in waves.

Josh pressing against my clit, set off a torrent. I looked up during a lull in the waves and saw his eyes were scrunched, biting his lower lip as if in pain. I realized he was holding back, waiting for me to cum again. How long he had been delaying his own orgasm, I wondered.

"I want you to cum," I said, digging my fingernails into his ass. He groaned what sounded like Thank God, but I cannot be sure, because when his first hot thread exploded inside of me, I came again.


I was groggy when I woke up the next day. We made love three more times and did not fall asleep until the early hours of morning. At some point, Josh must have returned to his own apartment, because the other side of my bed was empty. The sex had been better than I could have imagined. Sometimes he was tender, but at other times he ravished me with naked hunger.

But I was glad he had left before I woke. I needed to figure out what last night meant. Was I ready to risk heartache and give love a second chance, or would we just be friends with benefits? I needed to decide what I wanted and quick. Just avoiding him was not an option. Living in the same building, we were sure to run into one another and I could not afford to move.

Before I could think any further, I heard a crash, it sounded like it was coming from the kitchen.

Josh

By the time Savanna came into the kitchen, I had already swept up the broken platter and deposited it in the trash bin. I was picking shells out of the scrambled eggs when I smelled smoke. I was too late to save the bacon. It was burned to a crisp.

She took the steaming, mug I handed her and sipped. "Well at least you make a good cup of coffee." She surveyed the wreckage, but there was no anger in her eyes when she spoke, in fact she was smiling. "It is very sweet of you to want to make breakfast, but didn't we agree after the lasagna disaster, you wouldn't try to cook by yourself?"

I looked at her sheepishly. Both of us knew I was a mess in the kitchen. "But it's what couples do. Cook breakfast for each other."

She recoiled at the word couple and I panicked. "I didn't mean that we're a couple, unless you want us to be, of course. It's not like I'm suggesting we move in together. You still have six months left on your lease. I just—you know thought." Mercifully, she ended my rambling by putting her fingers to my lips,

"You are adorable when you're nervous. Come on, let's take a shower and see where things lead from there."

Where things led, where the bathroom floor, the kitchen counter, living room sofa and eventually back to Savanna's bed. It was 2:00 in the afternoon by the time I went back down to my apartment. I had seven missed calls from tenants all claiming they needed emergency repairs. I put on my tool belt and went to work whistling.

It's not like we went from one wild weekend of sex to being a couple. I had to work for it. It took time to convince Savanna, she

36

could trust me. It helped that we were friends long before we slept together.

Despite protests that she was not ready for a relationship, we spent most of our free time together. Still there were times when I could feel her pulling away.

When that happened, I gave her space. There was a two-week span where I did not see or hear from her at all. Eventually she showed up at my door, saying she had missed me and thought that was a sign we should be together. From that day forward, I never saw a sign of having any doubts.


On Sundays we would go to my parents' house for dinner. On Friday and Saturdays, we hung out with her teaching friends. My chest swelled with pride the first time she introduced me as her boyfriend. So, I was surprised when her lease was up, and she resisted moving in with me. I thought her trust issues were behind us.

"Even if I agree, I still want to keep my apartment."

"It would just be a waste of money."

"That's easy for you to say. Your name would still be on the lease if we broke up. I would end up homeless again."

I assured her I had no intentions of breaking up. She stayed adamant on the subject, until I pointed out if she banked the money she save on rent, she would have a deposit for a much better apartment in a nicer neighborhood, if at some point, decided she wanted to move out,

We moved her stuff into my place the first weekend in September. I had seen things turn bad, quickly, when couples moved into the building and lived together for the first time. But there was no friction between us. We did not even have an argument until November. That was when I took the call from her parents.

Savanna never gets angry, but when I told her they had called and invited us down for Christmas, she was adamant about not going. When I said, 'I already promised we would be there,' she had a fit and did not speak to me for two days.

I am not stupid. Savanna is keeping secrets from me; I just don't know what they are. I try to be understanding, because I have a secret of my own, that I would like to keep in the past. But this trip was about family, not secrets.

Her reluctance to visit her parents made no sense to me. I told her she was being unfair, pointing out that we had been together a little over a year and in that time, she had met my entire family, even cousins, and gone out clubbing with my sisters on several occasions. Yet I had not even met her parents. When I asked if it was because she was ashamed of me, she finally relented.

Not wanting to go to Key West in December made no sense to me. Mid-West winters can be harsh, and I hate the cold. To me a week in a sub-tropical climate sounded like paradise. So why was she so mad that I had accepted her parents' generous offer?

It did strike me as odd when her parents offered to pay for a hotel, since my understanding was that they owned some sort of guest house, but I did not question it.

I should not complain, the sex is phenomenal, and I know Savanna cares for me. But I am at the point in my life where I am ready to settle down and commit. It just seems, for her something is missing in our relationship. I haven't figured out what it is or how to give it to her. Hopefully, these next few days will help me discover what I can do to make her genuinely happy. Our flight leaves tomorrow.

# Secrets Revealed

Savanna - December 20th

Josh was just coming out of the shower when I got back to the room. He had a towel wrapped around his thick waist and was drying his sandy blonde hair. The walk back from the cafe had done little to dampen the burning desire between my legs. I ripped the towel from his waist and stripped out of my clothes in record time.

"I don't know what brought this on, but I like it."

"Don't talk, just lay back and enjoy the ride." He was already hard, and my pussy was dripping. There was no need for foreplay. I crawled atop him and lowered myself onto his thick shaft, giving out a long moan when he bottomed out. His large hands instinctively found my broad hips.

I leaned down to kiss him and my hips rose until his head almost slipped out, I gently lowered myself back down, savoring every contour of his magnificent cock. Our tongues entwined, his hand slid across my ass, the other at the small of my back, holding me close. He whispered in my ear, "I love you."

It was a very tender moment, and I wished I could enjoy it. But I am not sure I am at that point yet and my body was begging to come.

I kiss him passionately to keep him from saying any more and move my hips forcefully, grinding from side to side. Soon he is thrusting upward, meeting my every movement. I am panting with hunger and our bodies are quickly bathed in sweat.

The tenderness is gone and now Josh is firmly gripping my hips, guiding me up and down his hard cock, as heat radiates from my core. I lean forward, supporting myself with a hand on the mattress and move more rapidly. The orgasm is building inside me and to help it along I grip a breast and pinch its hard nipple. A long groan escapes my lips when I feel Josh swell beneath me. My walls are already tightly wrapped around him, but I squeeze hard and increase the friction between us.

I know he is close and pinch my nipple again, coaxing my orgasm to the surface. Josh spasms and electricity ignites my body as I feel the first thread coat my walls. The feeling of euphoria eventually fades, but he is still inside me. His movements brought on tiny afterquakes, causing me to giggle and roll off. I wrap an arm across his chest and kiss him on the neck. We lay there in silence until Josh speaks. "It's okay that you don't say it back."

"I'm just not ready. There is no denying I have powerful feelings for you, but I thought I was in love once before and was wrong. I don't want that to happen with us." I kiss him on the forehead, "When I say it, I want to be sure I mean it."

I know it probably sounds hypocritical to say this, with all the secrets I am keeping, but I just can't fully commit to someone who isn't a hundred percent honest with me. And Josh is keeping secrets of his own, something I realized the first time I met him.

We saw my parents' home, a block before we arrived at their doorstep. The two palm trees in the front yard were wrapped in colored LED lights, both the lower and upper porches were outlined in white twinkle lights. Lighted garland and wreaths hung from the railings. It was beautiful.

I told Josh, "My dad always made sure that we had the most lights of any house on our street when I was growing up."

As I got older, I started helping him. Those days after Thanksgiving, just me and him hanging the lights and drinking hot chocolate are one of the things I miss about having my family close to me. When my mom opened the door, the aroma of gingerbread filled the air.

My parents greeted me with warm hugs. Mom beamed. She was wearing a green blouse and white slacks. My father enveloped me in a warm embrace. The heat has not dampened his love of ugly Christmas sweaters. This one is covered in green and red palm trees. It is clear they are trying hard to make Christmas like it was when I was a kid. I decided, I too will make an effort.

Mother took one look at my sun dress and said, "You must be freezing in that outfit, come on inside where it's warm."

"Mom, it's 72 degrees out."

"I know. We will find you some heavier clothes for the rest of the week." Clearly my mother and father had acclimated to the heat of their new city better than I had ever been able to.

"You must be Josh," Dad said, extending a large hand. "I am Savannah's father, Flynn. Can I get you a beer?" he asked, leading Josh behind the check-in counter, where he keeps a mini fridge.

Someone opened a door to the foyer, and I heard laughter and Christmas music. It sounded like a large crowd. It reminded me of the amazing Christmas parties we used to throw back in Indianapolis.

*Wait a minute. I wonder what kind of party it is.*

I have never told Josh about my parents' unconventional lifestyle. And although they have promised to keep it quiet while we are here, I don't trust them. Ever since they opened the resort, it's like they have no boundaries.

"Just one night, is that too much to ask?" I hissed at my mother, "That you go one night without having a bunch of swingers here."

She gave me a soft smile and looked at Josh, who now had a beer in his hand. "I want you to meet some of our friends." I glared at her. She looked back at me with a sweet smile and whispered, "Our very vanilla friends."

She led me to the great room, while my dad showed Josh the outside of the house. This made me incredibly nervous; dad has a way of speaking without thinking first.

Mom guided me from group after group and I could not decide whether she was trying to convince me how normal the people were or impress me of her stature in the community. Most of the guests in attendance were area business owners or elected officials.

"Jack, I would like you to meet our daughter Savanna. She is a teacher back in Indianapolis. Mr. Stanley is the president of the school board."

"It is a pleasure to meet you. I've heard so many good things about you." Before we could continue the conversation, his phone chimed, and he excused himself.

Other than my parents the only person I recognized was my mom's best friend, Chloe. They roomed together at college and remained friends. I am surprised to see her.

"Oh my God Savannah you look beautiful, What's it been, 5 years?"

"Yes, ever since my parents moved down here. Are you living in Key West now, too?"

"Oh gracious no. I am a Georgia girl through and through. I'm in Atlanta and before you ask, yes I'm still single." She gives out a throaty laugh. In all the years I have known Chloe, she has never had a boyfriend. "What about you? I see you brought a date, is it serious?"

"His name is Josh," I say. "Is it serious? I don't know. He is a wonderful man but being back here has stirred up emotions I thought I buried when I left."

"Brock?"

"Yes, I ran into him yesterday." Changing the subject, "How often do you make the trip down here?"

"About every 3 months." Rita used to come up to Atlanta occasionally but hasn't made the trip in at least two years.

"I know the feeling. She hasn't come to visit Indianapolis since they moved here. It is like she has forgotten all about me."

"I feel bad for her. Mango Cove was never part of her retirement plan. In fact, she had been against it. But you know how your father is when he gets an idea. Rita adores him and against her better judgment, she went along."

I had no idea my mother felt that way. I had always assumed it was her idea to open a place to entertain her swinger friends. But it was what Chloe said next that got my attention.

"Now that Flynn's condition is getting worse, more and more of the responsibility falls on her."

I looked at her in confusion and she could see I had no idea what she was talking about. "It was good catching up. We will talk more, but now I need to help your mom in the kitchen."


Dad and Josh were still outside. I needed to find out what was wrong with him. There was also the fear that my father might accidentally reveal the true nature of Mango Cove. I gasped in wonderment when I stepped into the courtyard,

Even though mom had assured me they had no guests booked for the week, Dad had decorated the courtyard. White lights adorned the trees and bushes. Candles floated on the water of the pool and the hot tub was ringed by luminaries. The waterfall was lit from behind with blue lights. The sound system was playing Mannheim Steamroller. There were even wreaths hung on the doors of the tiny cabins which surrounded the courtyard.

Josh and my father were sitting at one of the round tables, under a brightly lit orchid tree, drinking beer. "It is beautiful Dad," I said, giving him a warm hug. He smelled like bayberry.

"It was my vision, but Brock did all the work. I don't get around as good as I used to, and he has been a tremendous help."

He looked around wistfully. "He put the Gulf Queen into dock early this year. Claimed the shrimp had moved to deeper water, but I think he did it so he could help with the Christmas festivities."

"Who's Brock?" Josh asked.

I looked at my father nervously. "Just a friend of the family." I answered, but there is no silencing my father.

"He's more than that. Brock is the first friend I made when we moved here, and I count myself as lucky for it. That young man does so much for the people of this town that nobody ever knows about. He also is the best shrimper in all the Keys."

"Is he here tonight?" asked Josh. "He sounds like an amazing guy. I would love to meet him."

"No, he was invited, but said he had other plans." I look at my father in surprise and he winks at me. I breathed a sigh of relief—then he continued, "I think the real reason was he's afraid Savanna might not want to see him."

I see the look on Josh's face and answer his question before he can ask, "We dated briefly. It wasn't anything."

"It was to Brock," My dad chimes in, not helping the situation at all. "A guy as good looking as him, could have his choice of any man or woman he wanted, but as far as I know, he hasn't been on a date since you broke things off with him."

Josh tilted his head, and I could tell it took him a minute to put the pieces together. "So, your ex-boyfriend is bisexual?"

I did not answer him. I was too stunned by the thought of Brock being hurt by my leaving. Does he love me? If so, why did he not ask me to stay? But now is not the time for these questions, "Come on, let's go inside, I am sure Mom is wondering what happened to us."

"You are probably right. She will be eager to introduce you and your new beau to our friends. She doesn't get many opportunities to entertain. We are both so busy running the resort." He sighed, "If I could find someone to manage this place, I would hire them tomorrow."

I noticed when Dad stood, he was a bit wobbly, and it irritated me that he had already had too much to drink. Then I saw he was drinking a Bud Zero. I reached out to take his arm, "Are you okay Dad?"

He waved me off, "I am fine I just stood up too quickly is all." But there is something in his look that told me otherwise. He looked so much older than the last time I saw him. I gave him a hug, "I'm sorry I stayed away so long Daddy."

"You are here now. That is all that matters. It is the best Christmas gift I could ask for."

I wanted to ask my mother about Dad's health and what Chloe had said, but when I got into the house, a cluster of people were gathered, listening to Mr. Stanley.

"—She has retired effective immediately." The little group murmured their approval.

*"Good for her."*

*"She so deserves it."*

*"I am sure she will do so many good things with the money."*

"What's going on?" I asked an older, heavyset woman next to me.

"Pixie Rolle, a teacher at the high school, or rather she was until tonight, She just called Jack to resign." I was a little confused why a teacher's resignation should create such a buzz. Realizing she left out the best part, the woman continued, "She won the Florida lottery and is moving back to Nassau."

"Oh, how nice. Have you seen my mom?"

"The last I saw her she was in the kitchen. You know, everyone is so excited for Pixie, it hasn't hit them yet that we are going to need a new English teacher when school starts again."

"You know Savanna teaches English back in Indianapolis," chimed in Josh.

"Her mother has mentioned it once or twice." She gave a laugh. "Or maybe it's more like a thousand times. She is so proud of you. Both of your parents are. I know they miss you."

"Josh, can you excuse me? I need to find my mother. I want to ask her about something." The plump woman gives him the once over and assures me she will be happy to keep him company.


The kitchen door was closed but I could hear my mother's voice inside. Rather than walking in, I stood there for a moment, listening.

"I worry about him Chloe. He was not a young man when we bought this place. I tried to talk him out of it, but you know how he is."

"That is the thing you love about him," Chloe said.

"It was a challenge, but we had contacts in the lifestyle community and soon the place was booked every week. I will not lie. We had a ball back then."

Chloe giggled. "Amazing times."

"But now that we're older, it seems like so much work. We spend all our energy catering to the needs of our guests. We barely have time for each other. Neither of us has been with another person in over two years."

"Is that such a terrible thing? Not being with other people, I mean?"

"No, that's not the point. I am happy with my sex life." I cringed. "I just wish I felt that way about the rest of my life. I miss Savanna. I always hoped she would follow us down here after she graduated from college, but in the year, she spent with us, it was clear she did not approve of our lifestyle and wanted nothing to do with us anymore."

I was stunned, I had no idea she felt that way. I just assumed there was no longer a place in their lives for me. All I ever wanted was for them to make time for me. Now I see it was the resort which took all their attention, not their lifestyle.

"If you are no longer interested in the lifestyle, why not convert Mango Cove to a traditional guest house and find somebody to run it for you?"

"You make it sound so simple." My mother sighed. "We have been looking for the right person to run this place for over a year. We just haven't found anyone we trust. If we don't find the right person soon, we may have to sell."


Back at the hotel we were getting ready for bed. 'I can't believe you didn't want me to meet your parents. They are absolutely fantastic."

"Um, huh." My head was spinning. The evening had thoroughly thrown me for a loop. There was so much to think about, not the least of which was my father's revelation about how Brock felt.

"All of their friends are so nice and that Brock sounds like one hell of a guy. Your dad really likes him. I hope we run into him while we are here."

"It is not likely." I said.

"Maybe you should call him. I would like to meet him."

"I don't think that would be a good idea." I rolled over and pretended to sleep.

Josh-

December 21st

Savanna wanted to pick up a few gifts for the people she worked with, so she and her mother roped me into going to the shops near Mallory Square. The sun felt good and not for the first time, I thought how nice it would be to live here year round. From what I had seen so far, the locals were very laid back. It was probably a long shot, to even try to convince Savanna of the idea.

But why not? Maybe a fresh start in a new place would do us both some good. Six years after finishing my MBA and I was still managing the shitty little apartment complex we lived in. And even though she has never said anything, I can tell Savanna is not exactly thrilled with the school she is teaching at. The dropout rate is high and many of the other teachers are older and have given up on the idea of being able to reach the students.

I was not paying attention to where we were going and bumped into a guy coming out of Sloppy Joe's. I had about thirty pounds on him and when we collided, he took the brunt of the impact, spilling Christmas presents across the sidewalk. I apologized and bent down to help him pick them up.

He gave me a dazzling smile, "My fault. I should have been more careful. I have a lot of pickups to make today and wasn't watching where I was going."

Rita and Savanna had not seen the collision and were a good hundred feet ahead of me, before they turned and came back to where I and the good-looking stranger were loading his packages into the bed of a dusty old truck.

"I can't believe it is collection day already." Rita said, "Time seems to go quicker every year."

"Collection day?" I asked.

"Where are my manners? Josh this is Brock, an old family friend and an absolute godsend." Even beneath his tanned skin I could tell he was blushing. He shook my extended hand, and I felt a stirring at his soft touch. It was a feeling I had not felt in years.

"Rita, if it wasn't for you, there wouldn't even be a toy drive."

"Wait a second. Are you saying my mom started this thing?" I had forgotten about Savanna for a moment. When she spoke, I quickly let go of the other man's hand.

"It is not a big deal. It was a suggestion I made at the Chamber of Commerce the first year we were here. The local bars have boxes set up for people to drop off presents for kids who are not as well off as some of us. Brock picks them up a few days before Christmas and the local charities and police deliver them to families that need a little extra help.

"Your mother is being modest," Brock said. "She has organized numerous benefits to aid local charities."

Rita waved him off. "Enough of this chit-chat, we have shopping to do, and Brock has a bunch of pickups to make."

Savanna had been sniping at her mom all morning and I was eager for a break from their bickering. I also hoped getting to know her ex-boyfriend might help me understand what she is not getting from me. I looked at his soft green eyes and asked, "Would you like some help?"

## Savanna

Still standing on the sidewalk, trying to figure out what the hell had just happened. Josh was spending the afternoon with my ex-boyfriend. What could possibly go wrong there?

And my mother had a whole volunteer life that I knew nothing about. A fact that did not fit with the self-centered image I had of her. But the question that needed to be answered the most was, "Mom, what is going on with Dad?"

"Whatever do you mean?"

I stared at her, with my hands on my hips and she broke, "Fine, I will answer all of your questions, but let's get off the street." We ducked into a restaurant on one of the side streets and after ordering a couple slices of key lime pie, my mother was ready to talk.

"It started during your junior year of high school. The doctors said it was an auto-immune disease." She went on to explain, while not life threatening, it caused mobility issues and low energy levels. The specialists recommended a warmer climate because his condition is made worse by cold weather.

"We had vacationed down here for so many years, it seemed like the logical place." My father was highly successful in his business dealings, and they had more than enough money for him to retire early."

"Why did you never tell me any of this?"

"We didn't want you to worry. Besides, he thrived in the warmer temperatures, so there wasn't anything to tell. But you know your father, soon he was bored with all the free time on his hands and convinced me we should open Mango Cove."

"Was it a swinger's resort when you bought it?"

"No and we had no intention of it becoming one. By then we were older and did not play with other couples as much as we used to. From the beginning it was just something to spice up our marriage. We didn't have romantic feeling for the other people we slept with, but overtime they became our friends."

She went on to explain, the idea had seemed nice at first. A guest house where they could host their friends when they were in town. But word started spreading and before long they were getting calls from people, they did not know. They all wanted to stay at Mango, and dad never turned away a paying guest. It just snowballed until they were running a full-blown lifestyle resort.

Tears were leaking from my eyes.

"Savanna, I know you do not approve of some of the things your father and I have done in our private life. But that is in the past. Neither of us has been with another person, in over three years."

"Mom," I sniffled. "That is not why I am crying. There is something I must confess. It has never been your lifestyle that I objected to."

"Then why did you always seem so angry with us?"

"I thought you moved down here because you chose your swinger friends over me. But now I know you were just doing what was best for daddy's health."

"Oh Savanna." She put her hand on my arm. "We would never choose anyone over you. Your father and I, love you more than anything in the world."

"Have you really not been with anyone other than dad in three years?" I hesitate, "Even Chloe?"

She does not look surprised by the question. "How long have you known?"

"I've suspected, but you just confirmed it." Rather than being ashamed that I knew her secret, my mother seemed relieved. She told me how it started during their freshman year of college and

52

continued for years after she married my father. He was aware of it from the start and although he was never intimate with Chloe, the three of them shared a special bond. "I was in love with both of them and they were accepting of it."

"So, you think it is possible to love two people at the same time?"

"I know it is," she said. "You would be surprised at how many committed threesomes we have visit Mango Cove. They are looking for a place where they can vacation without being hassled about their unconventional relationship. Key Wester's are the least judgmental people I have ever met."

I tried to imagine the trust and open communication a relationship like that would require. Something I had struggled to find with one man, I could not see how it would ever work with two of them.

Besides, Josh was straight and would never have any interest in being with another man. But that did not mean I could not fantasize about it. Which is exactly what I did when I returned to our hotel room and saw that he was still out.


Josh


Brock's truck, like most vehicles I had seen in Key West, was an older model. Faded paint and a thick coating of coral dust, so I was surprised by how clean the interior was. I detected the faint odor of brine, not surprising for someone who made his living the way Brock did, but there was another scent. This one was far more pleasant. Fresh limes mixed with a rich earthy smell.

I looked around for the seatbelt and Brock said, "Don't worry about it, our first stop is just up the block."

"Then why not walk?" It seemed like a silly waste of gas.

"We need a way to haul the presents. You are about to discover the generosity of this town. Some years the truck is full before I finish picking up all the donations. I have to unload and make a second trip."

"It sounds like a lot of work. You do it every year?"

"Giving of oneself is not work, as my dad used to say." He looked at me, and I thought there was a look of sadness about him, despite his smile. "Here we are, let's go see what Rick has for us."

The guitarist stopped playing and spoke before my eyes adjusted to the dark interior of the bar. "Hey everyone, Brock is here collecting for the toy drive."

He strummed a little fanfare on the beat-up guitar. "I am going to pass this tip jar around while I help him load his truck and I want you cheap bastards, to reach deep in your pockets. Real deep, the money is going to a good cause."

"Carl, you didn't have to do that." Brock told him. "The toys are more than enough."

"It's the least I can do after you helped me put on the new roof. Who's your friend?" Brock introduced me and together the three of us hauled a surprising amount of packages from the back room out to the truck.

When we got back inside, a busty waitress handed Carl a fat envelope. "Put this money to good use."

Brock promised he would and then shook hands. He stopped at every table, greeting most of them by name. It was the same at all the stops we made. People seemed to love him.

After two hours, the truck was almost full, and I was starting to understand what Savanna saw in him. In addition to his incredibly good looks, Brock was warm and sincere. Everywhere we went people had a story about how he had helped them out of a jam or lent a hand when they needed it.

"I hate to say it, but I think we need to unload the truck."

"How many more stops do we have," I asked.

"Just one, but every year they have the biggest donation." Why don't we take this over to the collection point and then I can drop you off at the Island House."

"How do you know where we are staying?"

"Flynn tends to talk a lot. Probably more than he should."

I laughed, thinking of my conversation with the old man the previous night. "You mean like when he told me you used to date his daughter? I thought Savanna was going to kill him."

"Yep, he really has no boundaries. That's why I like him so much."

There was a large group waiting for us when we arrived at the Conch Center, and it did not take long to unload the Ford. I enjoyed spending time with Brock and was in no rush to get back to the hotel, so I offered to go with him to the last bar.

"I am kind of a regular there. They will probably want me to stay for a couple of drinks."

"Sounds great to me. I could use a beer." I gave him a wink, "Unless you are tired of me."

"Not at all, you are good company," he said with a smile. "I am not sure you will be comfortable that is all. It is a gay bar." He stared at me, watching for my reaction.

"Is the beer cold?"

"The coldest in town." He smiled and put the truck in gear.

The bar was halfway between the ocean and Gulf ends of Duval. The sun had set just before we got there. The neon sign above the entrance to the Merry-Go-Round bathed us in purple light. Two elaborate carousel horses stood outside the front door. The sounds of tech-no pop coming from inside were loud. Looking through the open windows I could see there was already a decently sized crowd.

Brock said something I could not hear. He leaned in closer, and I caught a whiff of the lime and earthiness I had been smelling all day. It was his cologne. Damn he smelled good.

Speaking louder this time, "I said are you sure you are okay with this?" I was touched by his concern and nodded that he should lead the way.

I could tell from the wide exterior that the club was large. It took up most of the block. But I did not realize how massive it was until we were inside. I could see three separate bars. Brock led us to the one to the left, it appeared to be mostly locals and an older crowd. As was the case everywhere else we had been, he knew them all by name. They greeted him with enthusiasm.

I felt someone staring at me and turned to look. His dyed black hair was done up in a pompadour. A look at his face told me he was no stranger to cosmetic surgery. The name Lenny was stitched in royal blue on the pink fabric of the bowling shirt he was wearing. He asked Brock, "Who's your friend?"

"This is Josh, he is helping me with the collections. Speaking of which, I need to find Phil." Before leaving, Brock gave the old man a wink. "You two behave yourselves while I am gone."

"You're not from around here, are you?" Lenny asked, taking my hand in both of his.

"No, I am just in town for the holiday. We are visiting my girlfriend's family."

Dropping my hand, he gave out a dramatic sigh. "Girlfriend? Why is it that all the good ones are either married or straight?" Laughing at his own joke he went back to his martini, just as Brock came back.

"Phil's guys should have everything loaded in a couple of minutes and we can get you out of here."

"There's no rush. Besides, you promised me a cold beer." In truth I had never been in a gay bar before and did not know when I would get another chance like this.

"Okay. Sounds good." He indicated a couple empty stools at the bar.

I pointed further back in the building, to the area jammed with bodies, watching the male dancers in tight shorts or briefs, perform atop of the bar. "Why don't we sit over there." His eyebrows went up in surprise but said nothing.

I will meet you there." Brock said before heading to the restroom.

One of the dancers whipped out his meaty cock, and the crowd cried out. When the patrons started shoving bills into his G-string, the other dancers followed suit. Soon dicks were wagging up and down the bar. Gaping at the package on the performer in front of me, I could feel my mouth watering. His cock was thick and heavily veined. He moved toward me but at the last second gave a well-practiced spin and moved on to the man seated next to me.

It was a fantasy land. So many cocks, each of a different size, color, and shape. And nobody was judging me for looking at them. I was lost in euphoria for a moment when Brock tapped me on the shoulder. I turned, hoping he had not noticed I had been seconds away from trying to deep throat one of the dancers. Maybe I could play it off.

"This is crazy, did you see how close that guy got to me." I shook my head in mock disgust. "Like I really wanted to see his dick up close and personal."

"Does Savanna know?" he asked.

"I have no idea what you are talking about." But I could see by the look in his eyes, he knew the truth. I weakly asked, "Are you going to tell her?"

"No. It is not my place to interfere in another man's business. But if you want to talk about it, I will listen." I nodded, and he led us further back into the bar, through a door, and onto a patio area.

There were couples and small groups of men seated at the tables, scattered around a horseshoe bar. The night air felt good after the heat of the crowded club. Brock ordered us a couple of beers and we found a table away from the others.

"I am not gay, if that is what you are thinking" I looked down at my hands. "Somewhere about my junior or senior year of high school, I realized I was attracted to guys as much as I was to girls. Not that I had much of a shot with either sex. I was pretty nerdy back then. It wasn't until college that I had an opportunity to act on that attraction."

"It was my freshman year of college. His name was Frank. He lived in the same dorm as me."

Brock silently sipped his beer. "We were both just coming back from classes. The weather was still warm, and I thought nothing of it, when he asked if I wanted to go swimming at the old quarry."

"When we got there, Frank stripped out of his clothes. He had played varsity sports in high school and was very muscular. I left my shorts on, so he would not see my growing erection. We dove into the water."

I paused and looked at the surrounding couples, holding hands, expressing affection for one another. It was an environment like nothing I had ever experienced in Indianapolis.

"When we came up out of the water, Frank swam over and kissed me. I kissed him back and on shore, allowed him to remove my shorts. It was the first time I got a blow job from a man. And it was amazing."

I waved to the bartender for another round. "My parents were extremely religious and for the next few weeks I worried I was going to hell. I screwed every girl who would let me, trying to convince myself I was straight."

Brock had not said anything since we sat down. I huffed in frustration. "Are you going to say anything? I am telling you my deepest secret and you sit there like one of those Easter Island statues."

"I don't mean to sound unsympathetic, but what is the big deal? I've known since I was young that I like both men and women. It's just who I am."

I started to object, but he continued. "I understand it might be more difficult to be out in the open, up north. I am lucky to have grown up in a place as accepting and open-minded as Key West. But if you want to be happy, you must be true to yourself—and honest with Savanna."

"But I don't want to lose her, I love her so much."

"Why do you think you would lose her?" He seemed genuinely confused.

"When I asked her why she broke up with you, she said there were things she could not accept. No matter how much I pushed she wouldn't tell me what it was. When I discovered you were bisexual, I assumed that was what she was talking about."

He choked on his beer. "It was not my sexuality that was the issue. Far from it."

He did not explain any further, and I sensed it was pointless to push him. We finished our drinks and Brock dropped me off at the hotel.

Before getting out of the truck I thanked him for being such a good listener and without thinking, leaned in to kiss him on the cheek. But ended up kissing him on the lips. We both pulled away but not before things had gotten heated. I grabbed for the door handle and got the hell out of there.

My heart was still racing when I got off of the elevator. My cock was throbbing, but Savanna was already asleep. I knew it was pointless to try to wake her. The woman could sleep through an earthquake. If I wanted relief, I would have to take matters into my own hands.

Stripping out of my clothes, I climbed into bed next to my girlfriend, and fantasized about what her ex might look like nude and stroked my rigid shaft. I have a vivid imagination and it was not long before my balls contacted and sprayed my stomach with warmth.

## Brock

I pulled out of the parking lot before Josh was even through the lobby doors. I drove around for a while before parking near the break wall at Smathers Beach. The moon rising over the ocean usually has a calming effect on me, but not that night.

I slammed my fist against the steering wheel, angry at what I had almost allowed to happen with Josh. It would have been the ultimate betrayal of Savanna.

I knew her strong feelings about fidelity. It would have destroyed any chance she and Josh had of happiness.

I am not the type of man who makes excuses for his bad behavior. If I were, I might point out that it's been two years since I have experienced physical intimacy of any kind.

Or that Josh is exactly the type of man I have always been attracted to. Athletic without being hung up on his appearance. Funny, in a dry wit kind of way. But what I found sexiest was his willingness to show vulnerability.

It could not have been easy for him to share his fears and desires with me. It is a characteristic I do not have, which ultimately led to the end of my relationship with Savanna.

When I was in the third grade, I came home, and my mother was not there. My dad very calmly and simply explained she had left and was never coming back. After that, he never talked about her again.

He was a good man, but not one to show emotion. It is a trait he passed on to me. I cannot recall him ever telling me that he loved me. As I said, he was a good man, and showed love in his own way. That was enough for me, but some people need to hear the words.

Maybe if I had told Savanna how much I loved her and did not want her to leave, she would have stayed. But like I said, I have never been good at expressing my feelings or emotions. It's just not how I was raised. I am sure Josh is the type of man who tells her he loves her every chance he gets.

I resolved to avoid both of them for the rest of their visit. There was no need to further muddy the waters between them.

Pulling myself back together, I had a chuckle over his concern that she might leave him, because of his bisexuality. On more than one occasion she had talked about her desire to see me with another man. The idea was a turn-on for her and me too.

When I asked her how she could square her desires with her strong feelings about infidelity, she quoted something I had heard her father say many times:

*"Love makes us want to share our life with one person. Share our innermost thoughts, our dreams, and aspirations. We work together to build a family and raise children. Love does all those things, but it does not keep us from wanting to sleep with other people. Ethical non-monogamy gives us an outlet for these urges with no one getting hurt."*

"In other words, it is not cheating, if everyone is on the same page," she finished with a smile.

I was feeling better and hoped she and Josh would find their way. I cared for both and wanted them to be happy.

I dropped the truck in gear and headed home. It was late, and I needed to get some rest. Flynn was having problems with the hot tub at Mango Cove, and I planned to surprise him by repairing it while he and Rita were in Homestead.

# *Shared*

December 22nd

Josh

I awoke the next morning to find the bed empty. Savanna was not in our suite, and I feared Brock might have told her what happened the previous night. That she had been repulsed or jealous and had taken another room in the hotel. Or maybe she just decided she liked Brock better. Hell, maybe she was with him right now.

I breathed a sigh of relief when the door opened, and Savanna came in carrying two cups from Marino's.

"Hey sleepy head. You were out late last night. Did you have a nice time?"

How much did she know? I wondered. I took a deep breath and decided I had to tell her the truth before she heard it from Brock. Although she was the only person I had slept with since meeting her, I still needed to be honest.

She deserved to know I am bisexual. But first I wanted to know more about her relationship with Brock.

"Your old boyfriend seems nice." She just stared at me, her hands on her hips.

"Oh, come on. I know you and Brock were once an item. Your father practically admitted as much the other night."

"Yeah. It was a long time ago." She was staring at her coffee cup.

"I think he still has feelings for you." I watched her closely for a reaction. "Maybe you have feelings of your own."

"Let it go Josh," she begged. But I did not stop. If I was about to confess my secrets, it was time she shared hers.

"What was it like dating a bisexual man? Were you afraid he was going to sleep with another dude? Is that why you broke up with him?" I knew I was being a dick, but wanted to make her angry. Maybe then she would drop the wall and tell me what really happened.

"Fuck you Josh." She was pissed now. "If you must know, he just wasn't that into me. When I got the teaching job back in Indianapolis, he never asked me to stay, never told me he loved me."

She started crying, and I felt like shit. I tried to hold her, but she pushed me away.

"You want to hear the laughable part? I was the one that suggested other men." She looked as if waiting for me to respond, but I was too stunned to say anything.

"I thought it would be hot to watch him suck another man off and convinced him to invite a friend to join us." My dick twitched, but I said nothing, and she continued.

"All three of us took turns with one another, then they teamed up on me. It was the best sex I ever had." Savanna glared at me, challenging me to speak.

"I thought Brock was into it just as much as I was. He never complained at the time, but clearly, he was repulsed by my slutty behavior." Tears were streaming down her red cheeks. "Is that what you wanted to hear, Josh. That I'm just a skanky little slut and that is why Brock never said he loved me and the reason he let me go so easily."

"Brock doesn't think you're a skank and neither do I. In fact, he is still in love with you."

"How could you know that?"

"When I tried to kiss him, he pulled away saying, it would be a betrayal on both our parts."

"You tried to kiss him?" If I thought she was pissed before, it was nothing compared to the anger I saw in her eyes now. "What the fuck, one day in Key West and now you're gay. And want to cheat on me with my ex? It doesn't make any sense."

"I have no plans of cheating on you, and I am not gay. But I am bisexual. I'm sorry, I should have told you a long time ago."

"So, making out with someone, isn't cheating to you?" she sneered at me. "Good to know."

"I can't explain why it happened. Being at the Merry-Go-Round, must have brought out a side of me I haven't explored in a long time. Brock was a good listener."

I could no longer read her expression, so I kept rambling. "I just got swept up in the moment. It didn't mean anything. I have slept with other men—before I met you. There has been nobody since, male or female."

She did not say anything for a long time. I could not tell if she was jealous, hurt, or angry. When she finally spoke, there was a calmness to her voice. "I love you."

I was not sure I heard her correctly. She had never said it before. Closing the distance between us, she wrapped her arms around me and whispered again, "I love you."

"Because I'm bisexual?"

"No, because you are finally being honest. I have loved you for a very long time but held back telling you, because I knew you were keeping a secret from me."

Before I could say anything, she kissed me.

## Savanna

Maybe it was the thought of him kissing Brock or maybe it was because I had just told Josh that I loved him, for the first time. Whatever the cause, I desperately needed to feel him inside of me.

"Make love to me," I whispered.

He quickly had me pinned against the wall. I wrapped my legs around his waist. He kissed my collarbone, nibbled my neck, and fondled my breasts. His hard cock found my needy pussy and drove deep inside. I was so turned on; it did not take long to orgasm.

I was still trying to catch my breath when he carried me to the loveseat and spun me around, bending me over the back. This time, he took his time. When his head touched my seam, my whole body quivered. He teased me, rubbing himself up and down my slick lips. I needed him inside of me again. Looking over my shoulder, I snarled, "Fuck me."

When he slammed home, I let out a gasp. He was so damn hard. I wondered if he was thinking about me or Brock. When he grabbed my hips and thrust again, I decided I did not care who he was thinking about. I just wanted him to pound me with that thick cock.

Matching his every thrust, needing him as deep as possible, we fucked hard. I felt another orgasm building in my core and let Josh take control. He knew my body well.

Pulling me back against him, he increased the pace. The air was alive with the sounds of our grunts and groans, and the slapping of our flesh.

His balls grazed my nub each time our bodies collided. Every thrust made me wetter. I contracted my muscles, to increase the friction.

When he moaned, 'cum for me.' I lost all control. The orgasm was explosive, and I exhaled in exhaustion. Josh carried me to bed, and we slept in one another's arms.

I awoke a couple of hours later and Josh was next to me. His head propped in his hand, just watching me. A wiser man might have considered himself lucky and been content that I had forgiven him. But Josh is not a wise man.

"I don't believe either of us has anything to be ashamed of," he said.

"I think it's best we just leave those things in the past and move on," I told him.

"But is not what I want, and I don't think you do either. I like guys and girls, and last night helped make me okay with it. I want us to do what you and Brock did."

"What are you talking about?" I asked, even though I already knew what he was hinting at.

"The thought of having a threesome with you and another man has occurred to me more than once, but until today I was terrified to bring it up."

"Not going to happen Josh. Sorry. I promised myself I would never risk ruining another relationship that way."

"But you didn't ruin it. Do you still have feelings for him?"

"Yes. Yes, I do. Seeing him the other day made me realize that, but I'm in love with you, Josh. After this weekend we'll be back in Indianapolis and can put this all behind us."

He did not look happy, but I wanted there to be no chance for either of us to run into Brock. "Why don't we just spend the whole time in bed."

"That doesn't sound like a great way to spend our time in Key West. I want to get out and see the sites. Plus, the pool here is always crowded." I shook my head, but he wasn't done. "And what about Christmas? We have to show up for Christmas dinner at your parents' house."

"I'm sure we won't run into Brock there. There's no way my mother would be stupid enough to invite him. She knows things did not end on the best of terms with us."

As if she knew we were talking about her, my phone played "The Bitch Is Back."

"You really need to change your mother's ring tone."

I was tempted to ignore the call but knew, she would just call right back.

"Your father and I have to go to Homestead today."

"For what? That's a two-hour drive each way." With holiday traffic it would be more like three hours.

"Gustavus' is sold out of fresh turkeys. Can you believe it?"

"Buy a frozen one then." I heard her gasp at the very idea of serving a frozen bird at Christmas.

"I thought you and Josh would like to use the pool while we are gone." She huffed. "But remember, don't turn on the hot tub until your dad gets it fixed."

"Thanks for the offer, but I think we are just going to hang out at the hotel today. Please be careful. Highway 1 is going to be crowded. Don't let Daddy wear himself out."

"Don't worry. I will be doing the driving." Before we hung up, we told one another we loved them.

I paced the length of our suite. What a mess. I knew if we came to visit my parents we would run into Brock. I knew it would cause problems. How could it not have? No matter how much I tried to deny it, I was still in love with Brock. But I also loved Josh.

Under any circumstances, things would have been awkward. But I never could have imagined the situation I now faced. My current boyfriend was attracted to my former lover and from what Josh told me, the interest was mutual.

Key West may be a small town, but if I put my mind to it, I was sure we could avoid Brock for the next few days and then we would be back in Indianapolis. Once back home, Josh and I could put the whole thing behind us. Next year I would insist that my parents come to our place for the holidays.

I walked out onto the balcony. After a few moments of staring at the crowded pool area, overflowing with children, I had a thought. Brock would be tied up getting things ready for tomorrow's toy giveaway at the Conch Center.

I found Josh sulking in front of the TV. "Grab a bag. We are going swimming at my parents' house."


For a place that attracts visitors from all around the world, Key West is a small town. The entire key is just two miles wide and four miles long. Most of the tourists flock to Old Town, at the eastern end of the island. The walk down Whitehead St. from the Beach House to Mango Cove was less than a mile, so we did not bother with a taxi.

When we reached the Courthouse Deli, I debated stopping for a scoop of their banana split ice cream. I wished we could get it back in Indianapolis. I turned to ask Josh if he would like a scoop and found him across the street watching the chickens.

He was watching two roosters sparring with one another. Josh asked if they always fought like that.

"They seem more aggressive than normal," I told him, just as a loud squawk came from the tree above us. I looked up and pointed at the hen.

"That's what has them so riled up. They're fighting over her."

"Dumb birds, fighting over a woman." He gave me a wink, "They should just share her, instead."

A heard a voice coming from my subconscious moan, *'Mmmmmm, Now there's an idea.'* Quickly another voice, much shriller than the first screamed, *'NO. NO. NO. I will not allow it.'*

*'But they are both so fucking hot.'*

*'Shut up slut! It is your fault we're in this predicament to begin with.'*

*'But things are different now. It could be fun.'*

A third voice chimed in. "—Savanna, Savanna?" It was Josh. "You looked like you were a million miles away. Is everything okay?"

"I was just thinking about how much I love you." Taking his hand, I smiled.


We turned left at the Mile Marker Zero sign and my parents' place was on the right. Using my key, I let myself in and grabbed a couple of beers from the mini fridge, before joining Josh in the courtyard.

He was already naked. "What are you doing?"

"The resort's website says the courtyard area is clothing optional."

I was caught off guard. I had no idea Mango Cove had a website. It had to be my mother's idea. Dad could barely work the reservation system let alone build a website and then it hit me.

"Oh my God." I felt my ears getting red. "You know the truth then. That my parents run a swingers' resort."

"Yep," he laughed. "It sure helped me understand why you were so adamant about not wanting me to meet them."

"It was more than that. I mean I hated this place, but I hated them too. Especially my mother." I explained how I thought they had abandoned me for their lifestyle friends. Then yesterday I learned the truth. The move down here was for my father's health and not to be closer to their friends.

The warm climate did wonders and soon he was feeling so much better that he became bored with all the free time on his hands. Instead of taking up a hobby like fishing, in typical Flynn form he went looking for an opportunity to make money.

"Yeah, your dad told me all about it when we were out here the other night." Josh said. "Even offered me a job."

Nothing should surprise me by now. I knew my parents were looking for someone to manage the resort and Josh has a degree in Property Management. But I could not believe that neither one of them had said anything to me about it.

"What did you tell him?

"I said I would need to talk to you first. You know they miss you? He only offered me the job because they want us to move down here."

"I can't think about this right now." I am going to go for a swim and work on my tan. Stripping out of my bikini, I dove into the pool. When I came to the surface, I saw the hot tub was running and Josh was about to step in.

"Stop. Shut it off," I yelled. "Mom said to not use it until dad fixed it."

"I didn't touch anything. It just started going by itself."

That's when we heard the pounding coming from the pump house. Bam. Bam. Bam. "Somebody get me out of here. The door is stuck again." It sounded like Brock. Josh and I went to investigate.

Josh pulled the handle; the door didn't budge. "Sometimes it sticks because of the humidity," I told him.

"I'm going to pull from out here," he yelled to whoever was inside. "You push from your side.

After a lot of grunting and groaning, they had the door open. A very sweaty Brock emerged and averted his eyes. That was when I realized Josh and I were both still nude.

He handed Brock his beer. "You've got to be thirsty. Here drink this, I'll go get another one."

I wrapped a towel around my waist and apologized to Brock. "Mom said nobody would be here today."

He explained he had not heard us come in. While fixing the pump for the hot tub, a strong breeze blew the door shut. He did not realize it was jammed until after he had everything running again.

"I will get out of here so you two can enjoy your time alone."

"Don't be silly. You're here already, you might as well at least hop in the pool and cool off first."

He hesitated, and I saw uncertainty in his eyes.

"It's okay Josh told me everything this morning and I'm not mad." I hesitated, knowing what I said next would determine the future of mine and Josh's relationship. "To be honest, I wouldn't have blamed either of you if you had slept together. You're both so fucking sexy it is only natural you would be attracted to one another."

"No matter what you may believe, I love you and would never betray you that way."

There was a hitch in my breath. "I understand you are not very good at expressing your emotions, but is that really the only reason, you never told me you loved me until right now."

"What do you mean?"

"After we had sex with Carlos, you seemed different. Like maybe you were disappointed in me."

"No, I was disappointed in myself. Call me old-fashioned but I think when you sleep with someone there needs to be more than physical attraction. There needs to be an emotional connection. I had that with you, but not Carlos."

"Do you feel that connection to Josh?"

"I've just met him, but yes, I understand what you see in him. He loves you very much, and that is just one of the things we have in common.

Still naked, Josh came back with more beer. "Why aren't you in the pool yet? "Don't be such a stick in the mud. Get those sweaty clothes off," he said before hopping into the pool.

I saw no need for the towel since both men had seen me naked before and threw it on a lounge chair and joined Josh in the pool. Both of us watched as Brock undressed.

Needing time to think about what Brock had said, I swam laps. It really was a great pool when it wasn't full of swingers. When I finished swimming, Josh and Brock were standing in the shallow end, looking sexy as ever.

I reached the edge of the pool and rested my head on the deck. Kicking my feet back and forth in the warm water, I wondered what I had done in a past life to deserve the two of them. I loved them both and the affection they showed for one another seemed genuine. My eyes were closed, but I could hear snatches of their conversation.

"If you guys had not come along, I would have been in real trouble, it's like a sauna in there." I was thinking of other ways we could get sweaty. "It was stupid of me not to prop the door."

"Don't beat yourself up. It could have happened to anybody."

"That's two I owe you now. I don't think I thanked you for helping out yesterday."

"Oh, it was my pleasure," I heard Josh say. "I had fun hanging out with you. You're great to be around and I really like your company.

"I like you too. I can see why Savanna loves you so much."

Josh gave a laugh. "Well, I don't understand it. You're so much better looking than me. And popular, everybody loves you."

I had heard enough. Lifting my head, I said, "For God's sake will you two get it over with and just kiss already."

That was all the encouragement they needed.


As I watched, they embraced. Josh ran his hand across the other man's chest, softly kissing him on the lips. Brock wrapped his hands behind Josh's neck and pulled him close. Their tongues slipping in and out. I was growing more aroused with each expression of their desire for one another.

Brock put his hand behind Josh's head and pulled him close. Their hunger for one another was possibly the sexiest thing I had ever seen. Tongues slashing, lips sucking, mouths smashing. It was naked aggression I had never seen from either of them before. Hands dipped beneath the surface of the water as they fondled one another. The look on their faces hinted at the pleasure the other was giving him.

It was Josh who finally broke their embrace. "Let's get out of the sun. I want to suck your cock."

I exhaled a moaned sigh before following them to the lounge chairs set under a canopy of palm trees. I took the chair closest to where Josh was seated sideways. Brock stood in front of him, his magnificent rod pointing at the sky.

I could not pull my eyes away. I had seen it before, but never grew tired of its beauty. The shaft curved upward at just the right angle. It was tanned, like the rest of his body. At the top sat a fat pink head. It was longer than Josh's but not as thick. I fought the urge to take it into my mouth. There would be time for that later. Right now, I wanted to watch Josh suck him.

He wrapped his hand around Brock's shaft, measuring its girth before moving up and down its length. Brock gave out a groan. His pink head, moist with precum, disappeared before quickly popping up again in Josh's rapidly pumping fist.

My breathing grew heavy. A trail of wetness trickled down my thigh. I knew I would fuck both men before the day was over, but right now I wanted to see Josh suck cock.

Brock must have wanted it too, because he put his hands on Josh's head, and guided him to the pulsing tip. Licking his lips, Josh engulfed him. He bobbed up and down, rapidly at first. Then slowed, as he struggled to take it into his throat. Brock gave out a monstrous groan. Its vibration reverberated against my core.

"Oh God, that feels so fucking good." Josh sucked him deeper into his mouth. Brock's hips clenched, his legs went rigid, and he pulled Alex's head tightly against his pelvis. His breathing quickened, and he gave out another roar, before all the tension left his body and slipped down Josh's throat.

I wanted in on the fun and guided both men to the hot tub. I told Josh to sit on the edge and pulled Brock into the water with me. Standing between his thighs, I grabbed Josh's shaft, and gave Brock a sensuous kiss, before offering him a taste of the fat cock in my hand.

He did not hesitate to accept it and soon our tongues were playfully battling for the sweet taste of precum.

We ran our tongues up and down opposite sides of his shaft, pausing when we reached the top to share a kiss. Occasionally we took turns kissing Josh and I could taste Brock still on his lips.

With my mouth I sucked his head, popping it in and out. Brock licked his balls, flicking his tongue against the sensitive area, just above his asshole. Josh moved forward so that his hips hung over the edge of the hot tub and pulled his knees to his chest.

Brock wasted no time before slipping a finger into the tight hole. Josh gave out a pained groan when the large digit popped past his tight ring. Groans changed to moans as Brock worked his hand back and forth.

I stroked him fast, feeling the pulsing in my hand, I sucked him deep into my mouth. I did not swallow all the creamy warmth. Instead, I saved a bit to share with Brock, who greedily sucked it from my tongue. Looking up at Josh, he said, "You taste delicious."

With their own needs temporarily satisfied, they turned their attentions to me. After lifting me to the edge of the deck, they hopped out of the water and sat next to me. Josh on one side, Brock on the other, they were kissing my neck and playing with my chest.

Mouths soon found their way to my boobs. Josh layered soft kisses across the entire breast, while Brock sucked and nipped at a nipple. The difference in their approaches left me breathless and a little disoriented. It was not long before their hands worked their way to my thighs. I let out a little giggle and Josh asked if they were tickling me.

"No. I was just thinking about all the times my mother had told guests that there was no sex allowed in the hot tub. If she knew what we were doing, she would have a fit."

They smiled and said she wouldn't hear it from them. I was still laughing when I leaned back, letting them explore my folds. A finger parted my seam, and I stopped laughing.

There was a splash, and I wondered if one of them had fallen in, until I felt my legs being spread and thighs kissed. I kept my eyes closed, no longer caring which hand or mouth belonged to who. I was content to bathe in the adoration of these two sexy men, worshiping my body with theirs. Individually they were both incredibly talented lovers and understood my body well. Working in harmony, they brought me pleasure like I had never experienced before.

I had little time to come down from one high, before I was again being touched, licked or probed in a manner that took me to new heights. Nearing exhaustion, but still needing to be filled, I begged them to stop for a moment.

On shaky legs I walked to the table and took a sip of Josh's beer. The rough concrete of the deck had rubbed against my ass. When Josh noticed the redness he said, it would probably be more comfortable in one of those rooms.

I looked towards the cabin he had indicated and shook my head. "No way," I said. You have no idea what kind of things go on in those rooms."

"Things like a woman sharing her boyfriend's dick with another man? Those kinds of things?"

"I get your point and maybe I've been a little too judgmental of my parents' lifestyle." I grabbed them by their cocks and led them to the nearest cabin.

Once the door closed, they enveloped me in their arms. My body thrummed at the feel of their masculinity pressing against my bare flesh. I buried my face in Brock's broad chest. He smelled of lime, with a light hint of manly perspiration. Josh traced a finger from my neck down to my hip. His touch was soft and gentle.

In one smooth motion Brock gathered me up in his arms and laid me in the center of the bed. Looking up at them, I knew I would allow them to do whatever they wanted, so great was my trust in them.

Crawling in bed next to me, Brock kissed my forehead and looked me in the eyes, "Are you sure this is what you want?"

"More than anything in the world."

He then looked at Josh, who gave a slight nod.

When he entered me, I let out a contented sigh. It had been a long time since we were last together, but my pussy recognized the gentle curve of his shaft and clenched tight, welcoming him home.

Once he was all the way in, he leaned down and kissed me. Our tongues entwined, my arms wrapped around his back, tight walls gripping his long cock. I moaned in delight.

Then he pulled back. Already missing the feel of his cock, my hands gripped his firm ass, urging him forward again. He set a tantalizingly slow pace. It was clear he intended to make love, not just fuck. My pulse quickened as Josh brushed my cheek with the back of his hand.

Being with two men may not be every woman's fantasy, but it is my deepest desire. I kissed each of them. Then they kissed one another, Brock continued moving in and out.

My pussy was soaked with the need to cum. I lifted my hips up and down, urging Brock to pick up his pace. Warmth quickly spread. My nipples grew hard, I clutched Josh's arm. Back arched, legs wrapped around Brock's back; I rode the orgasm to its peak. He did not stop, but slowed, allowing me to catch my breath.

When my breathing returned to normal, he finally pulled out. I was glad to see he was still hard because we were just getting started. Rolling to my stomach, I raised up on my hands and knees.

"Josh, come kneel in front of me." I wanted to feel him in my mouth while Brock took me from behind. They exchanged a glance and smiled at one another. With their dicks filling two of my holes, they leaned in and kissed one another over my back. *Can this day get any hotter?* I wondered.

As if reading my mind, Josh pinched my nipples. Brock stuck a finger in my ass. I cried out. The feeling was a mix of agony and ecstasy, it was exquisite. I slammed my hips back against Brock and told him to slap my ass. Then took Josh deep in my throat. It must have taken a great deal of willpower for him to not come, watching as Brock and I fucked like wild animals in front of him.

"Don't pull out. I want to feel your cum in her when it is my turn."

Brock responded with a series of grunts and groans, driving deeper within me on every thrust. His relentless pounding made it impossible for me to keep Josh in my mouth.

I gave up and held him in my hand. Brock was nearing his climax; I could feel him growing harder. With one final grunt he filled me with milky warmth. When he pulled out. I did not have long to enjoy the sensation of his fluid running down my thigh, because Josh was quickly at my rear.

I purred and spread my knees wider in anticipation of his fat cock. Brock wrapped his hand around Josh's shaft, moving it up and down my slit. Coating it in our mixed juices. After he guided Josh to my opening, I expected him to kneel in front of me. But he had other plans.

He was licking at my clit, while Josh moved in and out. It was my biggest orgasm of the day.

I collapsed on the bed exhausted, and never so happy in my life. The slow rotation of the ceiling fan was the only sound. Snuggled between my two lovers I wanted to lie there forever. Brock said, "We better get out of here. Your parents will be back soon."

As if on cue, I heard my father's voice. "It looks like Brock got the hot tub fixed."

My mother said, "It looks like he left his clothes behind."

I cringed and wanted to die when I heard Dad say, "So did Josh and Savannah. That is her bikini top over there isn't it?"

"They better not have had sex in that hot tub." Josh and Brock both laughed. I pulled back from the window when my father turned in the direction of our cabin.

"Come on, let's go inside, I'm tired." Mercifully, he turned off the courtyard lights.

We snuck out like thieves into the night, gathering our clothes and getting dressed, before escaping through the side gate.

The men were not ready to say goodnight and suggested we head over to Duval St. In the bars, we danced, all three of us together. I kissed the men, and they kissed each other. And nobody stared, nobody cared. At least for one night we were free to express our love for one another. It was an incredibly liberating feeling, and I finally understood why my parents love this town so much.

It was the wee hours of the morning when we found our way back to the Beach House. The men were still raring to go. I was exhausted. "I am going to go lay down, but feel free to enjoy one another."

I could hear them undressing even before I had left the room. Leaving the bedroom door open a crack, I watched as they stripped each other with frantic need.

I watched as they embraced. Their mouths came together, hands traveled up and down. Josh gave out a moan, Brock was softly stroking his cock. Tilting his head back, he closed his eyes and murmured when Brock bent to kiss his chest. I leaned against the wall and dipped a hand into my shorts.

Brock spun him around and bent him over the spot on the couch, where Josh had fucked me earlier in the day. They were facing me, but had their eyes closed. Brock's cock nestled between Josh's ass cheeks; he reached around to grip his balls. I traced the edges of my puffing lips. By the time they moved to the floor, my folds were slick with arousal.

Brock placed his hands on Josh's thighs. He licked up and down the length of his cock, using the flat of his tongue. When his mouth closed over the tip, Josh grabbed at the couch. Brock was swirling his tongue around the twitching head of Josh's dick. He pulled off, allowing his saliva to drip downward to the crack of his ass.

Satisfied, he took him back into his mouth, while rubbing his hole with a thumb. I saw Josh's eyes go wide when the first finger entered him. At the second finger he gave a satisfied grunt. Brock released his cock from his mouth, focusing his attention on Josh's ass, putting a third finger in him. I stifled a moan, and slipped a couple of fingers into my pussy.

Satisfied that my boyfriend was stretched sufficiently; Brock withdrew his hand. He grabbed Josh's legs with his strong hands and spread them. The wide head of Brock's cock pressed against his asshole. Josh gave out a gasp when he pushed inward. I feverishly worked my hand in and out.

Josh pulled his knees up, to his chest. Brock moved his hips in and out. Both men were groaning, bathed in sweat. By now my hand was buried deep in my pussy, matching their rhythms. I was no longer tired, and needed release. Not wanting to intrude on the scene playing out in front of me. I rubbed my breast, pinching the nipple.

The orgasm tore through my body, spasms squeezed at my fingers, hips twisting, I cried out as my legs buckled. My pussy was still twitching when I sank to the floor. I watched from the doorway. The men did not notice, By their heavy breathing, I could tell they were rapidly approaching their own orgasms.

Josh pulled his knees tighter to his chest, wanting to feel Brock's full length. He cried out, "Fuck me harder." Brock obliged.

When Brock could no longer hold out, he withdrew his cock from Josh's ass and furiously stroked. There was a thunderous roar when he came, shooting heavy threads across Josh's belly and trembling cock. He ran a hand across Josh's stomach and used his cum to jerk Josh off.

Exhausted, I took one last look at Josh. Their mingled fluids glimmered in the light of the moon, through the balcony window. I smiled and crawled to our large king-sized bed. When the men eventually joined me, I was fast asleep.

The next day we met Brock at the Conch Center and helped with the distribution of toys. Seeing the joy in the children's eyes made me glad we had taken the time. In the evening we went down to the Bight for the festival of lights.

The area was ablaze in holiday glow. Boats shined in the harbor; their riggings covered in colorful lights. Fish traps were stacked and +decorated to resemble Christmas trees. Everywhere we went people were singing Christmas carols. Brock had been right. You do not need snow to feel the spirit of Christmas.

Christmas Eve was spent in our suite at the Beach House where the three of us watched *It's A Wonderful Life* and then took turns making love to each other.

Christmas Day

Savanna

Underneath the joy we felt in one another's company, there was a bit of sadness. Josh and I, would be leaving the next day. Having resolved things with my parents, I knew we would often return to Key West, still our hearts were aching. Brock came into the room and looked at us. He could read the sadness in our eyes.

"I will not make the same mistake again. Savannah, I love you, and Josh I have equally strong feelings for you. It is still not easy for me to show my emotions but I'm asking, begging you, please don't leave."

My eyes filled with tears. "Two years ago, those words would have made me the happiest woman alive. Now they just cause me pain because there is no way we can stay. Neither of us have jobs here. Our life is back in Indianapolis."

"Is it really?" Josh asked. "Were we this happy back in Indiana? Have you ever felt so alive as you have this week? I know I have not. We belong here Savanna."

"We've been through this already. Both of you are important parts of my life. but my career is also important to me. I am a teacher and there are no opportunities here."

I kissed them both on the cheek. "Let's just enjoy the time we have left."

They were disappointed, but knew my mind was made up and did not argue. "Come on, let's get dressed. I have a special treat for you after my parents' house." That seemed to cheer them up a bit. Now I just had to think of something we hadn't done already.

Mom did not say a word when Josh and I showed up with Brock. Dad just looked at us with a knowing smile and gave me a wink.

It was nice being there with my parents and the two men I loved. The thought that Josh and I would be heading home tomorrow made me sad. But there was no way we could stay any longer. Josh had responsibilities waiting back at the apartment building and I needed to finish my lesson plans before the New Year. We were kicking off the semester with a deep dive into the works of Charles Dickinson.

We had just finished dinner. Mom was about to serve dessert when there was a knock at the front door. "Who the heck could that be on Christmas Day?" my dad grumbled.

"It better not be a guest arriving a day early," Mom said. "I'll go deal with it. Savanna, would you mind slicing the pie while I'm gone?".

While we waited, Dad asked Josh if he had given any more thought to his job offer. He looked at me and I shook my head. As much as I knew Josh would enjoy it and wanted to help my parents, I was a teacher and there were no available teaching jobs in Key West.

Before I could speak, mom came in with a gentleman who looked familiar. "Savanna, do you remember Dr. Livingston? You met him at the party the other night?"

"I'm sorry. There were so many new faces."

"It's quite alright dear," said the gray-haired man. "I hate interrupting your holiday, and I would not be here if it wasn't an emergency."

He explained as Superintendent, he handled filling any unplanned vacancies. In past years there had always been someone available. But during the pandemic many people left education for other careers. And now with Mrs. Rolle winning the lottery and moving back to the Bahamas he was unable to find an available Advance English instructor. To make matters worse, she was also the adviser for the school's literary publications.

"We have several students we expected to win awards at next month's state competitions, but the committee will only consider entries nominated by an adviser. The deadline to enter is New Year's Eve. I know it is a great deal to ask on such short notice, but is there any way I could convince you to take the job?"

I looked at Josh and he smiled. Brock was smiling too, and they both were nodding their heads.

Tears of joy were streaming down my cheeks, when I said, "Dr. Livingston, you can tell the awards committee your school has a new English teacher."

Everyone was in a celebratory mood when we got back to the Beach House. Brock was ready for the after-dinner surprise I had promised them, but Josh wanted to make a phone call first.

"That is correct sir. I am resigning as property manager effective at the end of the month."

I could tell by the look on his face the conversation was not going well, and he might be on the phone for a while.

I looked at Brock and turned on the radio. "I guess we'll have to start without him."

Stepping onto the coffee table, I did a slow strip tease. Free of my sweater and bra, I swayed back and forth. Josh was still trying to get a word in edgewise, but I had his attention. Brock had taken a seat on the couch and watched as my pendulous breasts moved to the beat of the music.

I turned my back to them and bent over. Josh stammered, "Listen I have to go. Savanna and I will be back this week to clean out our unit." He hung up and joined Brock on the couch.

Turning back around, I ran my hands over the milky flesh of my belly. I cupped my pussy through the sheer silk panties. I could see that both men were hard. With a pillowy breast in each hand, I told them to get undressed, pinching a nipple between my red lacquered nails, for emphasis.

They were breathing heavily as I removed my panties. Stepping off the table I moved to the front of the couch. Placing a foot between them, I exposed my glistening pussy. "See how wet you make me."

I kneeled in front of Josh and took him into my mouth. Brock leaned to kiss him, while stroking his own cock. I replaced his hand with mine. Changing places several times, I sucked and stroked each of them. When I had them near their breaking point, I led them to the bedroom.

"Who gets to go first?" they asked.

"I don't think you understand. I want both of you. At the same time." Reaching into the nightstand, I handed Brock a small bottle of lube.

Josh pulled me into his lap, and I slipped my wet pussy over his erection. My hips were spread wide when I dropped down on his thick shaft. We moved our legs to give Brock room.

I gave out a long moan when his mouth found what it was looking for. His tongue at the top of my backdoor grazed Josh, and he sighed with delight. He slipped out of me and forced his cock into Brock's greedy mouth. After he licked it clean of my juices, he slipped it back into my needy cunt then licked my hard nub.

I leaned back against Josh, spreading my legs to give Brock better access, while continuing to ride up and down on the hard shaft.

When I felt his tongue against my tight pucker, a shiver ran up my spine, my hips rocked slowly in place. Beneath me, Josh let out a moan.

After squirting a generous dollop of lube in his hand, Brock coated my asshole and slid a finger in. When he put a second finger in, I said, "That's it, baby. Get me good and ready. Loosen up my tight asshole for your big cock."

Both men groaned, and I felt Josh twitch inside me. They love it when I talk dirty. Brock pushed his way in, and I gave out a pained cry. I had had each of them in my ass before, but this was the first time I had both holes filled and was shocked at how much pain was involved.

At my cry, the men had slowed, and I was wondering if double penetration was something better left to porn stars and the mind of smut writers. But then the pain disappeared, replaced by a feeling of fullness I never knew existed.

It took a while to find our rhythm. The sensation of their cock heads rubbing against one another, was indescribable. There was not a millimeter of pussy and ass that was not filled. My screams were now those of pleasure. Intense, indescribable pleasure.

Every nerve in my body surged with electricity. When I bore down, I could feel every contour of the men. They were growing aroused by my moans and cries and pumped faster and deeper. When orgasm finally overtook me, I lost the power of speech, only able to moan and sob.

When Brock came in my ass, I had another orgasm, causing Josh to release his own load, deep in my pussy.

When they finally went flaccid and withdrew, I felt an overwhelming sense of loss. Pulling them both close we dozed off and slept the sleep that only happiness can provide.

It has been six months since Josh and I, moved to Key West full time.

Brock kept the home on Caroline, but now shares a bed with us at Mango Cove. When he is not pulling shrimp out of the Gulf, he helps Josh around the resort. Their affection for one another has deepened with time. It is so cute watching them work together.

Dad is doing much better. He discovered that he enjoys fishing and can usually be found on his boat off the shores of Ft. Zach. Mom won't let him go out into open water alone, but sometimes he goes out with Brock and his crew.

He is very pleased with the changes Josh has made at Mango Cove. Even now, during the slow season, we are fully booked with polyamorous families looking for a place where they can vacation without having their relationships mocked. To my mother's relief, we still enforce the no sex in the hot tub policy.

Speaking of Mom, she has been nominated by the City Council as Woman of the Year, for all her hard work and support of local charities. She seems happier since turning her responsibilities at the guest house over to Josh. She now has time to visit Chloe in Atlanta once a month.

I love my new students. They took first place in the Scholastic Bowl earlier this year and most have accepted scholarships to colleges across the country. But I know in my heart they will all eventually return to Key West. There's just something about this place that gets in your blood.

I cannot imagine a better place for me and my husbands, to raise children. We are already looking into adoption.

Last week we sailed out at sunset and formalized our commitment as a triad, with a small ceremony.

## Find More Of My Work On Amazon

*I hope you enjoyed reading this story as much as I loved writing it for you. Your support is what makes me want to write more stories, so please **do this for me a favor**— Leave a quick review.*